A Den *of* Brigands

Novels by D. D. Cross

Field of Corns

Back to Hades: Eustice Seeney Returns to Hell

Go to Hell! (I DID) Interview With Eustice Seeney

Heapatrouble

A Den of Brigands

A Den *of* Brigands

D. D. Cross

MMA

Publishing

ISBN-13: 978-0615707648
ISBN-10: 0615707645

Cover art by Yuri Nasso from The Millennial Collection
Copyright © 2007

Beaufort Wind Scale: NOAA-National Oceanic and Atmospheric Administration United States Department of Commerce Library

Manufactured in the United States of America

10 9 8 7 6 5 4 3 2 1

Beaufort Wind Scale Developed in 1805 by Sir Francis Beaufort

Beaufort*	Avg Miles per Hour	Knots	Surroundings
0 calm		0-1	Smoke rises vertically and the sea is mirror smooth
1 light air	1.2 - 3.0	1 - 3	Smoke moves slightly with breeze and shows direction of wind
2 light breeze	3.7 - 7.5	4 - 6	You can feel the breeze on your face and hear the leaves start to rustle
3 gentle breeze	8.0 - 12.5	7 - 10	Smoke will move horizontally and small branches start to sway. Wind extends a light flag
4 moderate	13.0 - 18.6	11 - 16	Loose dust or sand on the ground will move and larger branches will sway, loose paper blows
5 fresh breeze	19.3 - 25.0	17 - 21	Surface waves form of water and small trees sway
6 strong breeze	25.5 - 31.0	22 - 27	Trees begin to bend with the force of the wind and causes whistling in telephone wires. Some spray on the sea surface
7 moderate gale	32.0 - 38.0	28 - 33	Large trees sway. Moderate sea spray
8 fresh gale	39.0 - 46.0	34 - 40	Twigs break from trees, and long streaks of foam appear on the ocean
9 strong gale	47.0 - 55.0	41 - 47	Branches break from trees
10 whole gale	56.0 - 64.0	48 - 55	Trees are uprooted and the sea takes on a white appearance
11 storm	65.0 - 74.0	56 - 63	Widespread damage
12 hurricane	75+	64 +	Structural damage on land, and storm waves at sea

National Oceanic and Atmospheric Administration United States Department of Commerce Library

SECTION ONE

Approximately thirty thousand feet above Homeland Security, a well dressed man with a professional demeanor, en route from the toilet back to his assigned seat stopped suddenly. He lost five shades of a deep tan, did a double take, and in an authoritative tone said: "We've got a problem."

He sprung across two passengers and yanked a woman from her window seat. Who was this weirdo, and why was he jumping on this young lady? The passengers didn't have a clue what was happening. The woman, stunned, braced herself for what was about to occur. She gasped, opened her mouth to scream, but was smothered by nearly two hundred pounds of muscle. Like a maniac hopped up on meth, he straddled her on the aisle. She pushed back hard, but not before he ripped open her sinewy blouse, and yanked the clasp off her front loader bra. He began inspecting the lower quadrant of her right breast and armpit. Just as he suspected, Steri-Strips covered the incision of recent implant surgery. With his thumb and index finger he tried separating the tissues, to no avail. He needed something firm to slit the subcuticular and deeper tissues. Looking over his shoulder the sight of a butter knife caught his eye. He grabbed it and created a gash large enough to work his hand into the site. Groping frantically he finally snared the implant leaving blood everywhere. The passengers gushed, oohs, aahs, and a whole lot of what the fucking hell is going ons! Looking at each other for a hero to emerge, one of the air hosts went for the attacker.

"Stand down!" The man shouted.

Chase ignored him and continued with what he'd set out to do. He held out the implant and yelled: "We've got a problem this is a freaking bomb!"

Something touched his chest. There was a screech like a cat was set afire, and a hiss that lasted less than a blink. A jolt shook the plane. An icy gust tore through the cabin. Everyone on board was too stunned to shiver, but stared at the man being transformed before their eyes. In an instant he was frozen solid. Passengers scrambled, some in horror, some transfixed by the sight of it. This would be a flight to remember. The thing that froze him? Damn that was a deterrent if ever there was one. The weapon's blast froze all movement immediately, but bits of perception lingered on. Death didn't pay a visit, this was suspended animation. Yeah Chase knew what it was. He saw himself in his mind's eye, unable to move, gradually losing consciousness, as neurologic pathways shut down. He saw the passengers collectively stare. Today wasn't their day to be terror victims. Sure their trip was disrupted, but no one could help being freaked out at the site of a man standing there frozen. A block of ice in the aisle of a jetliner. Thank goodness for airline security, the big bad criminal had been subdued. Yeah right, the frozen man would later recall. Some fucking criminal, I came here to save these assholes.

A few would later describe the frozen man with an equally iced breast implant, as a bizarre Rodin sculpture minus the bird crap. Fortunately a podiatrist on board stabilized the woman's wound.

The air host put away the freezing device. Now he had a gun pointed at Milton Chase. He whipped an ID from his pocket and flashed it around in that: I'm a Fed sort of circular way, so that the crew could see his bona fides. Then tossed it to a flight attendant.

At that moment a cackle, tap tap tap, and the intercom came on: "This is the captain," he needed to get a message out, calm the folks down, and let the sky Marshall know everything was under control.

A flight attendant passed along info about the unruly passenger. He wasn't a threat after all. The Captain knew Chase was an agent of the United States government. Half the plane caught on that the frozen guy was on their side, the other half remained too shocked, too pissed, or too drunk to move.

Except of course the sky Marshall. He was new at the job.

He would be remembered as an officious weasel who'd metered out some pretty hefty punishment. This was all spelled out to the passengers, who received complimentary airfare, and a few tailor made perks in exchange for silence, confidentiality, and of course their agreements to keep their mouths shut. This was done by beefy looking bureaucrats in dark suits with thin briefcases, who could express these sorts of things in a remarkably convincing manner.

So our sky marshal was armed with some nifty equipment. We'll get back to that.

Mr. Marshal was armed with the latest of weaponry a "Tetronic Freezare" a sort of cold laser, taser. The man, before being zapped into ice, was maybe a year or two too old to play a professional sport, and way to young to retire. He knew that the breast implant was set to explode when the internal barometric pressure of the jet hit full ascent at thirty-five thousand feet.

The calming Captain made everything right. As for Milton Chase, he'd remain in a cryonic state until the sorting out process was complete. After all he wasn't with the government very long. How long ago was it that this guy got to where he is today?

Not Too Long Ago, This Is What Happened:
Beaufort Scale Rising

Dr. Milton Chase finished off a mildly chaotic day by treating himself to a sunset drive along the coastal highway. The sea was calm and smoke would rise vertically. The car's motion through the still humid air made it sweep across his face and through his hair, which he usually kept tucked beneath a baseball cap worn backwards, whilst driving his convertible. His hair was long but not too long, he'd let it grow out since the Army. Buzz cuts made grooming in the desert easier to care for. Yep, MC was done with soldiering. Basic training sucked, close combat training stung, and war, shit. War is war. Patching up soldiers in a FST (forward surgical team) and all the hot air of a commissioned officer was done. Fuck it, the two year hitch paid off his student loan debt, and front line surgery honed his skill set. MC had to admit the uniform did get him laid, or so he thought, which wasn't often. It wasn't just the oak leaf clusters and ribbons rather his rugged good looks. Fuck that too. It was cool being an officer, but not cool enough to check back in after all. The Army's accommodations weren't exactly the Four Seasons.

Today marked one year in private practice, which as things go, went well. Life for MC is good and it's going to get better, he figured. Fiddling with the music system, enjoying the wind's caress, it enveloped the lines of the sports car as it pierced the dusk, like being in a wind tunnel. Maybe a two on the Beaufort scale (a means of measuring the wind) Cool. He would later recall just how good the air smelled, and the sky looked, when headlights showed up on his side view mirror. Immediately some jerk was on his six, honking. Tailgating bozo in a hurry on a quiet stretch of highway? Take the main drag, asshole. This ass face is gonna fuck with me? Florida road rage victims were a big part of his orthopedic surgery practice's success. He was not going to be one of his competitors patients. No. Not an option. He flipped the jag off the universal fuck-all sign, and slowed down. "So I'm an asshole. I'm a fucking war hero too." He saw the pickup truck behind him the driver had on a cowboy hat, white, and there was some sort of an insignia on the windshield.

Clunk! "Cocksucker rear ended me. What the fuck?" Milton hit the gas pedal hard, and all those cylinders put some distance between him and the truck. Where are the cops? Shit. There he was again, the white zone. More adrenaline kicked in, this isn't Najaf. His pulse, maybe a buck forty before he downshifted, I'm not in a war zone this is fucking Palm Beach. The truck was pushing in hard, bumping the sports car again and again. I don't want a fight, he repeated to himself, looking again at the truck. Shit, the guy had a gun. Chase punched it, the ragtop's tires screamed as he took a curve. He felt his pulse climbing, not gonna let that fucker land me in the red zone he was thinking, when BAM. The road blasted into a blinding prism of bright lights, and he hit the brakes hard. He saw the construction site's barriers as the car spun, and yanked the emergency brake hard coming to a halt in a patch of gravel. Shit. He ratcheted the ride out of the rubble ramping up the RPMs as he got back to the road. Time to throttle the fuck out of this no win zone. Shit, the truck was on him again. Fast like a freaking bulldog in heat. The asshole wanted a piece of him, but MC wasn't going to be anyone's prey, not tonight. He gunned the engine and scanned the terrain. Finding an angle, he took it reflexively jamming his foot on the brake pedal, this time cutting the steering wheel hard, burning rubber. The car barreled down a driveway of one of the mansions. He brought the car to a halt, revved the engine, readying himself in case the truck didn't keep moving down A-1-A, it's momentum carrying it past the turnoff.

Maybe the fucker would slam into the roadwork mess, and spend some time in lock down, when John Q got around to showing up. In the few beats he'd been readying the roadster, the trucker crawled up the driveway and was right on his ass. Its door flew open and the driver crouched a wide-legged stance utilizing a double handed grip on a weapon he'd prefer to have in his own hands. Chase's first impression was that this clown had done this before, and he might just shoot and actually kill him. He tried to think of something conciliatory to say, something full of reason, but knew better. Reason, sweet as it can be doesn't always apply.

Boom! Boom! Boom! Boom! Chase hit the dirt hard rolling for cover. Hearing the shots ping off masonry, statues, and his car. Shit my new fucking car, he thought, just as he heard the pickup's wheels screech and saw it spin off in reverse.

At that very moment, flashbulb intensity lights painted the grounds. A squad of armed men in suits surrounded Chase, and advised him less than pleasantly, to raise his hands above his head. The sirens in the distance made him wonder if these were cops or private security. One of the men frisked him slowly, like he'd done it professionally, carefully removing his wallet. He glanced at it quickly then tossed it back to Chase.

When the cops showed up, the men in suits evaporated. He didn't know that the construction site barriers had gone along with them, or why.

There was a dead man on the second floor. Ricochet after all can be tricky, sometimes lethal, the cop would later say. In a courtroom with an otherwise bored legal stenographer chewing gum and typing away Chase's fate was about to be decided by one very busy somewhat tetched judge. Having a packed docket with not enough time, and too many creditors, con-artists, creeps, and crooks to contend with.

A Shred of Proof

Prison they say is the second place where a man finds his true character. The battlefield not unknown to Chase was the first. The absence of the pickup truck, the presence of the gun along with Milton's ability to use it, made him not just the prime suspect in the reckless discharge of a firearm and death of Sheik Abdul El Kazar, but the only suspect. The Sheik, Chase would learn prior to a trial by his peers, was a very important albeit dead chap. El Kazar, had been instrumental in financing an array of nefarious endeavors, including factions not necessarily friendly to the US, and to a degree matters of National Security. The facts as reported by investigators were that Milton Chase: "Had no right to drive on to his property, and discharge a firearm resulting in death."

The mixed breed Nordic-Hispanic prosecutor may have tried the case, but conceded at the behest of folks above her pay grade. She appeared reflective of an overburdened justice system. To an insider the rush to judgement, to close a case quickly and without much fanfare, seemed odd to Dina Fuentes, a staunch litigator one year out of law school. The fireball presented evidence, that the weapon found on the grounds belonged to Milton Chase MD. He had no defense other than it was some sort of conspiracy. His gun was stolen, and so on. It wouldn't hold water with a jury. His attorney recommended a plea bargain but Chase said: "I told you what happened, and that's the truth. I didn't come this far to not be taken with more than a grain of salt. I didn't even know the gun was gone."

This deal was the only one on the table. With the prospect of two decades behind bars, having confidence in a jury system, his lawyer advised, was at best dubious.

Milton C knew that most Americans avoided jury duty with more effort than avoiding root canal. Dr. Chase had a decent slice of this patient population in his private practice, who would come begging for a medical waiver to avoid jury duty.

So Chase cut a deal. The judge, at his own discretion, decided that the young doctor was going to deviate from the plea bargain/settlement between Chase's lawyer and the prosecutor. In fact; the judge having a pissy day, opted to toss out the agreement and throw the book at him. Upon hearing the judges words the former Major Milton Chase of the US Army reserves, verily should be held to different standards, consistent, and consequent to his training. He should have known the ramifications of weaponry and the handling of such. Reflective of his military training, his behavior according to the evidence, was more than guilty. He confessed by way of the plea deal to the crime, and would be given the maximum sentence. Upon hearing these words Chase turned mushy in both knees, and a pallor spread, according to a description by his lawyer, to a shade approaching albinism. Shit. He was looking at lots of years, and knew that he had already acquiesced via the plea deal to a lesser charge, and didn't have a way in this imperfect legal system to take it back. Not with any shred of proof of his innocence.

The orange prison scrubs fit just fine, almost like the blue or green ones he wore in the operating room. That life was over. License pulled, assets depleted, a fiancé gone, and all the crappy things that happen in life kicked into overdrive. The prospect of spending the better part of his life with his Johnson void of the female encounter didn't sit well at all. Broke, a bit suicidal, jailed, and sitting in his cell Chase thought on his first meeting with his cell mate. Romeo Divine, AKA John Grant, the King of Africa.

Milton didn't take to prison life like most. He pretty much made the best of it. Taking the refrain from one portion of society to another, as a pause for meditation, reflection, relaxation, and exercise. He stayed to himself. A confrontation with a prisoner could turn sour, and MC being the mindful sort didn't care to have an extra few years tagged on to his sentence. He figured he could do some serious good behavior, no sweat.

However, the other inmates at Maximum Security Prison TMZ167 did not have like-minded intents. On the second day of the second week of a constant recurring dream, his peaceful conscious cocoon would dissolve. Instead of a butterfly, some other permutation of hibernation arose to meet the throes of incarceration.

It went down like this: Chase was awoken from his repose by the metal on metal crunch of his cell door sliding to a halt. He sat up with a jolt as if an IED had gone off. Soaked in sweat from his recurring dreamscape, pupils open wide, fingers tingling, memories of dreams washing away, as he waited his reverie evaporated. The image of how things would have gone if the fuckable little prosecutor wasn't on the other side. If the system didn't have the deck stacked as well as she was. It was lack of female companionship, and "T.O.Y." time on the yard, that Chase could have lived without. But this shit? Surprise visits? What the fuck? What was this about? The bulls, two of them, stood there on the threshold of his "house" with a chained man between them. The guards were grinning in that smarmy way, when they're fucking with a con.

"Meet your new roomy Doc?" One of the guards said, as the other uncuffed him and thrust the big dude holding his blankets and personal effects into the cell.

He finally was getting a cellmate. Two men in close quarters and not a word spoken. Not even a meet and greet. Just the simple nod that they were both stuck in a cell, and they'd keep to themselves. No more, no less. The minutes tiptoed into hours, then days, and the men only saw each other as outlines of human beings of no particular sort. Caged nonentities, phantoms of sorts, whose realities were defined by outlines of some luminous unknown. The only acknowledgment of each other aside from toilet privileges, were the accidental bump or collision, which resulted in a burst apart the way a cue ball scatters racked balls on a felt table. They were nothing to each other. Not two men in a cell rathe,r a pair of nameless, faceless, masses incarcerated, for neither knew nor cared to discover why. Doing their own time in their own way. No pleasantries no words. None, nada, zip, they just ignored each other completely until...

On this tenth day of whatever month of incarceration, and one week after being assigned a person to share his private, yet not so private space MC enjoyed the respite on the yard, from close human quarterdom. The day on the yard went as it always did with MC minding to himself staring at the blueness of the sky, and freshness of the air, alone. Until he wasn't.

"Hey shitbird." The sing-song tone came from behind.

Milton turned slowly not wanting ANY pulse of adrenaline, keeping it cool. He looked at the person attached to the voice.

So there he was, staring at some six and a half foot bald headed prisoner tattooed so thickly you couldn't see his skin. What a jag off, he thought. The big question mark above his eyebrows stood out on his bald shining head, on that sunny Beaufort 2 day. Chase looked away and shook his head.

"What you looking at bitch?" The bald man with the question mark said. He walked hip hoppily as if being in prison was a reward for some greatness. Baldy QM stood in front of Chase with his fists on his hips and spit on the ground next to him. The similarly clad group subtly cheered him on with raised clenched fists and snickers, and then went back to lifting weights. Milton would learn later that this was the "New Aryan's for Jesus Society" they were always at odds with the Keith Richardist's. Question Mark, Chase discerned was not the leader, but the main muscle for a squad of what he considered cretinous blowhards unfortunately equipped with serious fists and weapons.

"What's the question mark for? Don't you know what you are?" Chase said.

"I know what you are, bitch!"

"Give the man a microwave oven, a Mercury Montego, a Mazda, a Matador, a Mercedes, a monogrammed set of genuine fake Indian jewelry, and a baby's arm holding an apple."

"Fuck you pussy! You look like my new bitch." QM looked over to his crew. He held up a hand, snapped his fingers, and the clunk of free weights obeying gravity hung in the air like the stench of body odor, testosterone, and cannabis. A little action on the yard started its simmer.

"I'm gonna have an ass party and you are gonna have some fresh cock meat, honey boy."

"Okay, so we're not going to be having dinner and a movie?"

The onlooking bandits in various states of altered addled adrenaline charged sweat, muscle strain, sprain, and spasm ambled over and formed a circle around the men.

Chase squatted and placed his arms and hands over his vital organs: liver, spleen, kidneys, and waited. Knees bent ready and prepared for a thrashing.

"You're just where I want you sweetie." QM pulled his scrub pants down. "Come on bitch do me!" He moved closer.

The circle tightened and Chase said. "Go fuck yourself." He sprang from his squatting position hitting baldy beneath his chin with the crown of his head, hammered a one-two to his throat, pivoted, and heaved a round-house kick to his chest sending him to the ground.

"Motherfucker!" Baldy said, through moans and croaks. "You're a dead man" he retched, and began waving the other arm. "Kill the fucking bastard!" He rasped and spewed orders from the fetal position, still choking, drooling and coughing. "Get the bastard dammit!"

Then something happened, another circle formed around the circle. An orbit, a very well defined orbit, formed around the skinhead Nazis. They were very large muscular men of African descent. All of them grinning in that "kill whitey" way, that black dudes in prison wear on their faces when they're about to kick some serious ass. All of them waiting for a sign from, who Chase saw was his cell mate, Romeo Divine.

SECTION TWO

Cellmates

For a month neither of them made eye contact. Tension hung over them like a pair of testicles over lava. Eventually they saw each other as a pair of cons on the same side. When the "what are you in for" came up, Chase was as innocent as the next con. Romeo of course hesitated a bit. He had read Chase's jacket before he hit the cell. Most jails leave the folder on the cot of a newcomer, so he knew what and who Milton Chase was in for. As for Romeo, he rarely thought of himself in jail. When he did, he considered himself a political prisoner, and a big dude not to be messed with. When it suited him he also thought of himself as a direct descendant of the Solomid Dynasty. Claiming direct descent from King Solomon and the Queen of Sheeba, and could trace his ancestral roots through a series of intermarriages to a tiny island on Lake T`Ana in Ethiopia. He had genealogical charts tracing his lineage to the conquest of Hamite on the coast of what was eventually to be the Ethiopian empire. As his personal history has it Romeo, aka John Grant, ancestors refused conversion to the Christian Coptics of Egypt and were exiled. He could trace his lineage through the kingdom of Aksum, through the tenth century and beyond. He had charts depicting his Divine status, which would have placed him in his rightful regal place as the child monarch, if Haile Selassie had not been ousted in December of 1960. It was Major Megistu Mariam's Provisional Military Administrative Council, also known as the Derg, who took over Ethiopia, nationalized the country, and destroyed all records of the Divine dynastic history. He would use this credential very much to his advantage.

The Brothers left him alone. Chase did not know why and kept his guard up for a while, R.O.Y. as in rumor on the yard, was that Chase was some war hero, doctor, and murdering thug. As for The King, the Neo Nazi skins wanted his kind back to Africa. However, they left him much to his own device, even affording him a bit of respect. Maybe it was the British accent, and the fact that Romeo frequently preached that he was to return his brothers and sisters to the continent before abrogating the throne, for a democratic nation state. To the Skinheads this was the Jig Messiah. Shanking him would be a waste of a good weapon. A walk through the yard wasn't just civil quid pro quo, but more of a system of respect, among and within the tribes. Romeo, Milt would learn, was locked up for selling memories. He would use a permutation of the Freezare device combined with a rapid thaw, and neural extractor, to remove the neuro synaptic junctions of the brains of select individuals. He would sell the holographic memories to pervs, spooks, or whoever, for the right price. Nobody died they just lost a few brain cells. Nothing he thought could do any harm. However, things did go wrong.

"How the hell do you sell memories? How do you steal them in the first place?" Chase asked sipping liquor provided by his cell mate.

"So you really wanna know?"

"Yeah I do. Another shot of Juniper juice would make this more interesting." Chase held out his cup.

"That's some good gin."

"No worries." His cell mate seemed to always have an abundance of contraband. "What else do I have to do but tell stories?" Romeo said. "It wasn't a technical leap. After all; brain cell structure is somewhat finite. You know this. You're a medical doctor. The mind is very much a skeleton, if you will. Mappable pathways, which need only a stream of consciousness to make them flow. MI5 and your government had been working on this in the last century."

"I remember reading about it somewhere years ago, back when the cell phone epidemic exploded in the US. At least the Europeans had harnesses for their phones, but back then every schmuck in the states had to be on a piece of junk pumping electromagnetic beams into their parietal lobes."

Romeo pouring more gin, "Stupid Americans think everything is as they say it is, without thinking, but then again mon, Americans are not permitted to think with the daily monsoons of information and struggles to make ends meet. Its a joke it is."

"Hey, I served my country."

"For what? Truth, justice, and a way of life that resembles a comic strip? Look where it got you?" He asked and answered. "No place mon, no place. You'll see how things unravel. Think back about how many times you been lied to, and what led us into the wars, and the world of memory mining."

"Quick innovations popped up and cryogenics caught on with the affluent, soon to be dead, tumor set. Squash clinics were the rage, every surgical resident had to learn basic neurosurgery, because more people died from EM related tumors than from the wars. That's when freezing caught on, and from what I remember, it sort of dropped off the radar for a while. There were problems with the artificial blood." MC said.

"It never faded mon. More like brushed under the rug and politicized, so it could be used for reasons of state, or so they said. In America, things like that win elections," Romeo said.

"They weaponized a wonderful thing." Chase said.

"I don't know how wonderful, but you're right. Funding in the US was shot down. Not much later tampering with frozen humans became a criminal offense. The big companies that did it covered their asses, called it a 'Cryopath Search' a way to examine the workings of the human body post mortem. Kind of like the twentieth century cigarette companies."

"Another scam. I could use a smoke mon, how about you?" Romeo took out a pack of Kools and lit one up.

Chase continued, "I remember that early twenty first century shit, 'the freeze the brain and save the body movement' was making tracks to the moronic affluent. It was a joke of sorts, to freeze someone's head and pump in artificial blood, only to reanimate them in some uncertain ways. A living hell for some poor schmucks trapped in a useless body. A fucking life sentence in a crappy ass prison."

"Like the one we're in now?" Romeo said. "It was a good scam, but for the money they spent there are enough frozen dead people to populate Madagascar. And let me tell you, many quadrillionaires to spend the money too. You could freeze a brain, or a whole body, for an extra few coins. Problem was bring'n one back. Bleedin' technology wasn't up to speed. For decades scams floated about, promising to keep someone on ice until a cure came along. When the real technology came about the early confidence folks were already old money. Today you can keep one alive in a frozen state, and the thoughts and memories stored. 'Cortichips' that's what they called them back then. Some still do. I prefer the term we in the business use Mempacks."

"Cute" Chase said.

"It isn't in any way cute. It is illegal and for all practical purposes, the Freezare is to the world out there, your world, just another weapon. Not the tool it can be."

"Yeah, it is a good way to blank out some asshole." Chase said. "But it's only good at close range."

"You are so silly my friend. The mixed purpose usefulness is a quite guarded thing indeed. At least to chaps like you from the straight world. Politicize a great thing and look what you have. Another bloody secret to make money from its mixed purpose prospects."

"You can't just go freezing people for kicks man. It's a crime. When the public caught on all those news stories, ads, and commercials, shit! There were even demonstrations. People ranting about soul tampering, and devil worship, all that crap. Those were some weird times. On the other hand, freezing someone on the battlefield is more humane than a flame throwing blast. Just tip them over and they shatter away."

"This is a good smoke mon. Years ago I'd go to jail for even thinking of lighting up. All a scam. Just like the 'Cell Phone Plague'. The fix? Ha! This was a simple manipulation of the molecules. It was there all along, but there was so much money to be made in disease. You know this you are a medical doctor."

"I'm a mechanic. I fix broken and deformed bones. They haven't figured out a way for machines to do what I did yet." Chase said.

"Back then the politicians claimed that the EM waves were an act of nature, an act of the Lord, and that was that. Proposed studies got shot down vis-a-vis no funding. But when half of the government got sick along with millions and millions of people there was a need for answers. There were none." Romeo said.

"At least not any the masses were privy to right?" Chase added.

"No. The public was urged to pray because the spat of tumors was an act of nature. Knowledge of what the chosen were doing went underground to cure the leaders of the free world. Years went by and the politicos, royals, and well heeled claimed publicly, that freezing people to later restore them was against the will of the guy upstairs. Even though the rich and powerful had been donating dollars to deep pockets, gaining favor, and doing it all to cure their own decay, disease, and dysfunction." Romeo paused, rolled his eyes upward and took a deep breath before continuing: "That whole Megillah, to suppress the facts got a lot of support from the grass root faithfuls in America. Some politically plugged in reverend on the take, said that the juice that runs through the gears, nooks, crannies, and synapses, is unique to us all. The 'sacred sauce' was beyond human interference. But the tumors spread threatening the work force. Finally another zealous 'man of faith' with a medical degree and church ran a university laboratory. He was given a charge by the powers that be: find a scientific reason behind a cure for the masses that coincide with the political milieu. I should call it pseudoscience for the worker bees, keep them on the job. They found proof in a test tube. To cure disease was the work of man with divine rights. And a Nobel Prize was won legitimizing a myth. Why? They, the ruling folk said that drugs, alcohol, climate, and temperature, all per mutate the stream of consciousness, but the structures remain intact. The notion that there was no justification for man to tamper with the jobs of the cell phone industry wasn't working. Too many deaths. Yet to enter a world of evil, that's what they called it, was the domain of only the pure and well educated. Entering the mind was either the work of the Devil, or this new breed of religious science. To invade that mindfulness was evil unless it was done just so by anointed experts. Biblical scholars and stars of one faith or another, called it an unnecessary evil to heal the sick, and caved to the pseudoscientific brain dentists. Extreme religionists even tried to put an end to cryogenics, but there was too much big dollar interest in the game. And the high priest psychodentists, delved reverentially for the select few. The discoveries they stumbled upon were to many, a quirk of nature, to others a fantastic find. One of the hypothetical problems was that a return from full body cryo meant that the subject lost a sense of self. The proverbial question as to who provides the lighting of our dreams, made a lot of people wonder if fucking with it would be worth it. The politico-religious reformists called it some sort of blasphemy. But behind some very thick closed doors and sealed chambers a new level of control emerged, and charlatans inclined to take these discoveries public needed to be sacrificed."

"So I guess you got burned at the stake?" Chase said.

"In a way." Romeo said. "In a way my friend I was routed." His voice trailed off, and he stared blankly at the cell wall.

NECESSITY CREATES INNOVATION

The alleged King of Africa threw back his head and heaved a heavy sigh. He spoke in a firm, even, no-nononsense, regal tone: "Milton, most of the civilized world acknowledges advances in science. America's politics and secrets? Ha! All such very serious bullshit to the masses. But religion? Go to church, the right church, and make your prayers. Then go wear your religion like a badge or rank of how holy you can be for all to see mon. Then the big shots with their faith and reverence, leave half the country starving and dying because they ain't got no food to eat, or health care, and sell them poison."

"Poison?" Chase notched his head in that what the fuck manner.

Romeo continued: "Yes, morphologically farm raised creatures sliced up to look like food. Oh yes. I know how that system works I was a part of it. Hell yes, I was there for the money because that my friend is what it is all about in the US of A. Act reverential, obtain political power, dismiss science and evolution as the root of all evil, and then proceed to goose your so-called faith, play it up for your followers. The scam of it all. Such a lovely time-tested ploy only goes so far. The leaders who were caught, bathing in fruits of the true believers efforts, the church going people's money, their life savings, would from time to time be exposed. Sometimes the one's who paid for their own enslavement would catch on, and they did not like it one bit. The biggest con there ever was. Fool the good honest working people for so long and they find out it's all a hoax. The gullible become wise, angry, bitter, or they act." Romeo Divine looked around the cell, and slowly the features of his face coalesced into a tight mirthful grin spreading from his mouth to the corners of his eyes. He held out his hands palms up shrugged and said: "I acted."

"You were an honest working stiff like I was. A hack orthopedic surgeon putting in hip, knee, and finger joints. Right?"

"Do some research. The prison's computers allow access to search engines. I worked for the greater good of the corporations. I studied in London. Ha, the silliness of profiling someone by a search on the internet. The water's have been muddied, but the basic facts can not be changed. They were different times. Times when we had full access to the procedures and protocols of a selective technology. I had it made by 'straight world standards. As a scholar I even consulted professionally with New Scotland Yard and the SAS. Besides, your US secret clubs, many have been using cryo and extractions clandestinely for years. Cortichips are a great source of information especially for interrogators. That's how I started out."

"I preferred torture." Chase said. "I showed them pictures of my mother-in-law to be."

"Even though my entry into the educational system, you might hear, was somewhat dubious, I did advance and develop several modifications. The possibilities were limitless, I thought."

"Why didn't you just stay legit?"

"I saw the limits. Besides mon, some of us are just born to make more than the pittance of a public servant."

"You could have contracted out to one of the government contractors like the mercs, or infrastructure workers."

"Too much politics. Being paid as a private contractor meant being tagged and monitored. Like some creature set free in the wild only to be dragged in for a checkup every now and then."

"Money? You sold people's thoughts and souls for a few shekels?"

"You are one damned funny man. Of course I did. I love the good life. The big money is in other peoples thoughts not their souls. My marks 'subjects' if you will, always went back to the thing that made them who they were." Romeo continued.

"That being?" Chase asked.

"Scum sucking greedy vermin without a soul to start with. I'm selective. Passwords and usernames to bank accounts and the money is mine. What crime other than grand theft do I commit?"

"You're ripping people off man. You're still fucking stealing shit."

"When I steal from a thief?" Romeo held up the liquor container. Chase held out his cup.

"You're fucking with people's bodies man. You're freezing `em. That's fucked up."

He poured Milt another tipple. "Listen we are all just machines mon. You above all should know that. These were assholes who had it coming. I never robbed an honest man."

"So you're an avenging angel right?"

"Mon you steal from a thief you're a Robin-bloody Hood."

"Well fuck him too, but you're still a criminal. You fucked up someplace or you wouldn't be here right?"

"Mon, mon, mon. Let me tell you this, I did everything to preserve the original stream, you know the stream of consciousness, so they'd thaw out just swell. That weren't easy mon. Workin' in Newstern Europe and North America I was the quickest thaw-man ever!"

"But you got popped. What'd you end up with?"

"I'd have the Cortichips," Romeo held up the liquor in the 'you ready for more' sort of way bartenders throughout time have done when they're spinning a yarn.

"Sure, I'll have some more. Romes my man, the left over brain chips? What's that deal all about?"

"The chips mon" That's what the govvies called the tangential memory packets."

"How do they work ?" MC took a pull of his drink.

"Thought processes worked in a few ways: either the linear simple thoughts which imprint easily, or the complex emotional and psychologically charged conceptual pathways entwining themselves throughout the hemispheres of the brain. Those didn't take but a cinch to yank out. The street name for Cortichips is like I said a Mempack, and the secret to success is, the faster they thaw the better a return to complete homeostasis. Nothing but a few lost memories. It's an art you know. To someone as bo peep as you Mempacks are used every day, only you don't know about it." Romeo said.

"So my whole awareness of the world, all my memories, are fair game to a memory thief. My parents imbedded ideas, notions, disciplines, my education and relationships, all have the potential to be stolen."

"Yes and no. Some pathways are structural, to the point as being a part of your anatomy like your femur or lungs. Time of entry of the memory and the level of structural integration preclude one from an extraction. Relatively newer thoughts, ideas, and schemes, are still a series of neurons lining up, firing bursts of contemplation. Those are the memories or thought processes we can access. Anything deeper without the magnitude of a structure like that could seriously alter the person."

"I was born a subject of natural child birth but brought up cesarean, and all those years of study can't be taken away even by the best brain thief, or can IT?"

"If they were you'd know it, and I wouldn't be doing a very good job. Besides if I removed your ability to wipe your ass where would that take you? Some things are learned and to unlearn requires too many integrated pathways."

"Dude, I remember an issue that `someone' could stick in fake memories and make people do things they would't do. You know like kill people and shit, even kill themselves. You can't have an army of zombies. That was just jive? Nobody knew for sure what the gig really was."

"Mon that's why we're at war. You think people are gonna let some guy in power put a bunch of ideas in your head to forward some political shit, and not fuck people up along the way? I'll answer you without hesitation Abso-Fucking-Lutely. External bombardment from the media is commonplace, rogue implantation is done behind closed doors." Romeo hiked his chin up and raised his voice a few octaves, "Mon my extractions were always perfect, quite specific."

"Until they weren't." MC said. "So what happened man? How'd you fuck up? You must've screwed up the process someplace or another. I'm curious how did you do your extractions?"

"Fock you mon! I NEVER screwed up. I had MY way doin' things. I got my secrets. I know my shit. What you think I'm gonna tell you my secrets?"

"What am I gonna do wipe my ass with them?" Chase said sarcastically.

"Maybe someday you get out of here you may want to toy around with other folks thoughts. It works like this: The serotonin dopamine pathways, after an instantaneous mesenteric plexus freeze raise the pH of the GI tract. The brain juices stop. Makes it possible for the mark to go back to what ever it is that makes them. That was my bloody innovation. Mine!" He thumped his chest.

"Relax man." MC said. "That ain't my thing. Besides I'm not into fucking with people, and you fucked up some people. Probably some important people, probably people at the top."

"I don't hurt no people mon. The Rapidthaw, that's what preserves any resemblance to a conscience, and let me tell you there's very little of that at the top. Get in, get out, don't hesitate and reanimate. Nobody gets really hurt maybe just a little less smart."

"But someone did."

"Riddle me this brain thief how do you make money doing this shit?"

"Remember you can never rob an honest man or woman. Those with something to hide, some little scam, an easy route to riches, they are the perfect mark. Once you find that greed, that person with the urge, that hint of criminality, which lurks in all people you can sense it. When you do that you nurture it, drag it out, pander to their base instincts of getting something for nothing, or getting away with something. Once you do that you got them where you want them. The rest ha! The science? That's the easy part. So easy a retarded monkey could do it. The simplest and by far the least risky way is to find the best and most monied mark, meaning the buyer, who wants the thoughts from somebody else. Then we get close with them real palsy walsy, you dig, mon?." Romeo continued excited to brag about his scam world. "I had me a crew out there. My roper, someone who could identify with the victim. Ha! They're all victims. My man gains the vic's confidence, an easy scam to get in the door and steer him to meet the inside man. He's the bloke who ultimately fleeces him. The inside man comes next. Let me tell you, a good inside man is the key player. He stays near the mark gets to know him, and offers something. Promises anything the mark wants. A good inside man could listen to their stories for weeks, sometimes months. He'd finally give the mark a convincer."

"A convincer?" MC shrugged his shoulders. "What the fuck is that?"

"That is a process of allowing our victim a way to profit from a little side deal. The mark's in on a scam and he's diggin' it. He's gettin' to play dirty, and let me tell you everybody loves to get a little down and dirty, and gain that edge. Especially the rich and the powerful. Oh yes, that is how you gain his trust. We'd usually send in some little pleasure ploy chip. We'd sex them up and grift their skull in a hotel room, or at their home. The key to pulling off the brain scam is that when the mark goes to piss. That is when you make your move."

"As in urinate?" Chase said. "You fuck with the mark when they're taking a piss?"

"Of course, mon. That's the optimal time. When they go to piss they get that shudder of relief it's a burst of dopamine that enhances the pathways, and then I'd freeze them. Freeze them and drop a juice lid on their head."

"Juice lid?" Chase narrowed his eyes. "What the...?"

"A hat mon, more of a helmet of sorts. It's wired you know plugged in to a monitor the size of a bible. Transdermal infusers kick in like that!" Romeo snapped his fingers. "Immediately ionic plasma pulse kicks in while radio cellular transducers send back the signal from the cerebral cortex. I just punch in what I'm looking for and wait. Within a minute or so I'm watching their thoughts on the screen, and the holograph platform translates a three dimensional model of the brain cells. I hit a switch and have the structure in a pouch and shut off the infuser. I have my Mempack and that's what's sold."

"But it wasn't just that. You'd lift a few goodies for yourself right?"

"Sometimes. Sometimes this is when some problems could happen."

"Like what?" MC asked.

"When the heat from the infuser would start a thaw in the wrong place some bad shit would happen."

"How bad? I know this was done in labs, but you were doing this without all the gear in hotel rooms."

"I know. Hardly the sort of thing to be done in a hospital you know, witnesses and all. Lots and lots of questions. Just wouldn't happen."

"Government neurosurgeons used variations of what your describing on selective brain sites for years. It was after the C phone brain cancer epidemic. Standard medical procedure. I did the rotation and remember not only how boring it was, but the glitch. The fake blood didn't work as well as they hoped, and revitalizing the tissues even with hyperbaric assistance didn't cut it in the peer reviewed world of American Medical protocols. Just not enough oxygen got to the right places." Chase said.

"It's not in the freeze, it's the thaw. In and out like a thief in the night. Like I said mon we couldn't always do it in a controlled environment."

"No shit. The mere act of freezing an organism largely consisting of water formed ice crystals that became piercing projectiles of surrounding cells. The shit didn't work. Unbound H2O was the killer, and all memory was lost."

There was a loud crash like someone took a swing with a bat followed by reverberations that hung there for a moment. The two men were stunned but neither would show it. They both looked up.

"You two are awfully chatty in there. Keep it down." It was the guard who swung his nightstick like he was up at the plate. He would later recall how conversant these cons were about scientific things, politics, all sorts of crazy things. Things that had no place in the joint. "I don't know what you cons are cooking up,but remember this: I'm on to you. Get it?"

"We're just doing our time," Chase said.

"Thass all we's doin' massa." Romeo chimed in with his steppin fetchit.

"Open the cell door the guard hollered. "I'm gonna show you smartass crumbs what a good beat down feels like, and then we'll toss the cell for any contraband. I know we'll find something." He yelled out again: "Open the fucking cell up already!"

A strained hush fell over the cell block, like a fart on a crowded elevator. Nobody knew who or what, but something stunk. A blast of switches echoed throughout the cell block, and a guttural screech began to ratchet up louder and louder. Chase would later recall it sounding like a thousand cats caught in an elevator in hell. Then just like that the metal on metal whirring of the cell door drowned out the other sounds, and there he was. The crumb boss standing there with his weapon. A hush fell over the world and hung there like a dirty cloud of radioactive debris. An indeterminable period of time passed until the metronomic tap tap tapping got louder. Both men whose heads had remained bowed (everyone knows you don't look anyone in the face in prison) looked up. They looked at the uniformed man firmly beating his palm with his riot stick. He stood at the threshold of the cell's entry fury in his eyes, and a glint of joy that he might just be able to vent some hostility. That being one of the joys he took in being a prison guard. Twisted fuck the man was.

Not more than a second passed before a leg of the zealous guard was in the air, when another guard joined him. He put a hand on his shoulder and whispered something in his ear. The cell door did not slide shut, and the guard with the nightstick stopped his forward movement. He seemed to blush, but it was a brief burst of embarrassment as he turned to face Romeo and Chase. He stared at them like a hard ass who'd be back, before saying: "You caught a break today crumbs, but I'll be back." The two guards walked off and the cell block's murmurs and shouts ratcheted back up to it's usual pitch and cadence .

"What the fuck was that about?" Chase said.

"The bulls mon they treat us like fucking criminals."

"We are criminals Romeo."

"I am a political prisoner mon." He thumped his chest again.

"Keep it up douchebag," Chase muttered then glanced at Romeo and said: "I bet the prick's wife hasn't had any fresh batteries in a decade."

"I sold him a Mempack a few months back, and he's happy watching other people screw on his holopad."

"I can tell by the way he handles his stick. Back to this memory trade," Chase said. "Don't you remove things that might be needed?"

"Like I said, rarely."

"Tell me more about installing memories that don't exist?"

"That my friend will put you on death row. Putting a Mempack into someone is a rape of sorts. No, no, no, very bad business. Brain rape is very serious stuff. Mon I told you, the wars still are very much fought over these things. Don't you remember twentieth century stories about how some victim had bad childhood experiences? Brain screeners preceded what I can do now. You see, some things are real, and others implanted through the social milieu. Remember those big deal trials and tales of false child abuse?"

"Yeah used to make movies about that shit. Lotta phony cases went to trial too." Chase nodded. "Yeah some kid would rat out a priest or uncle because a Bullshit psychologist evoked some fake memories,"

"Memories? Mon they went further with technology. They put actual neurosynapitc pathways, ideas themselves, as real as real can be into kids heads to win court cases. Big money for a good brainscammer."

"They were doing it back then?"

"Shit mon. Reality is what happens even when you don't be believin' in it no more. A real biochemical pathway ain't gonna go no place once it's implanted."

"Shit." Chase said.

"What could be real and what could not? A lot of people believed things that never happened, and some psychonaut claimed some hypnotic truth. The Brainscreen was the first device to sort out what did or did not occur. The technology changed, went strictly biochemical. Only real memories remained after a good freeze and extraction."

"But removing real memories and selling them is okay?" The gin was effective. "I don't get it. The downside of stealing memories is that you forget a few things right?"

"Of course a few memories are lost, but mostly no one got hurt or went stupid."

"Tell me this Romeo..." His voice dropped a few octaves and Chase leaned forward. "Can you remove bad memories?"

"Oh yes mon." The King of Africa slapped his knee, grinned, and continued. "Milton that's easy. The cheapies in this game use brainscrubs the way people used party drugs." He looked at the liquor and notched his head, "or booze to forget. It's too easy and not enough loot. Dope and liquor are cheaper than a brainscrub. If you go 'high tech' something I've done a few times, a very delicate and selective removal of memories, the customer usually forgets to pay. I never care to deal with drunks or dopers. They always fock you mon."

"How come shrinks didn't pick up on it?"

Romeo spoke like he was delivering a lecture at a university: "Our society is based on a system that wants us to recall its past. Wholesale memory reduction would remove the guilt and shame some carry, and lighten the load of personal responsibility. It would destroy entire industries, and then some. Big govvies and good grifters have known about these things for years. Even some less than stellar doctors, whose moral compass is perpetually pointed wrong, use it for reasons one can only imagine."

"I still can't see how it works." Chase said.

"Listen do you recall Mandelbrot's randomness theory?" He didn't give Chase a chance to answer and continued, "Milton, do you think that the alcohol in that gin accidentally falls on the brain cells you want it to?" Romeo held up the container.

"No. It works because it saturates the entire central nervous system. But yeah I'm familiar with Mandelbrot.

He theorized about statistically recurring events, like tossing a hundred coins in the air and they all land heads up. Sure it could happen, but the procedure would take a gazillion years. A forever zone minus a super computer that says if enough rain drops fall on your windshield the Mona Lisa will be looking at you from over the steering wheel. Like a perfectly spun spider web. How many millennia did it take for them to get web making just right ?"

"There are ways to speed up those eons to make randomness predictable. Why am I here? I mean really here. Randomness theory revealed we are alive and here now, in jail. Its obvious I got caught not just with state secrets but worse. I made a lot of money and I have to tell you its a rush. Just picture looking at peoples memories, picking some for our own collection, and packaging those for sale to others. I had contracts to fulfill and many people wanted memories which did not exist for them."

"Makes porn seem wholesome." Chase said.

The prison's horn blared like a stage of Marshall amplifiers at a rock concert. This wasn't a stadium and it deafened some, paralyzed others, and sent earfuls of pain to all. The lights dimmed, flickered, and the cell block went black.

Seconds later another set of lights came, on red ones. The cell block's psycho ward chatter, shouts, manic laughs and screams, were drowned out by the horn, which, after a handful of repetitions finally stopped. All was still but for a dead silence and the slightest movements made sounds echo off the stone and steel. The silence bathed in bloody red light heightened the sense of imminent danger. Romeo grabbed Chase's upper arm and whispered: "Settle back and don't say a word the screws choreograph this for control, sometimes they do this before a shakedown."

"Isn't this usually yard time?" Chase eased back onto the cot. After a moment he leaned forward the mattress springs shouted out like the Sirens Odysseus must have heard. Shit. Chase had his elbows on his knees, his back tingled.

"They mix things up so nobody knows what's happening, so just be cool. mon "

"Romeo," Chase said softly. "If they do come here?"

No answer. Shit. The silence throttled Chase's cave dwelling fight or flight mechanism, but there was nowhere to run and how do you fight an armed jailer? Shit. Chase's eyes dilated, waiting. Time oozed slower than blood through a clogged vessel to the heart. Maybe this is why so many who survive prison even a short stretch, succumb to a fatal heart attack.

Finally the sound of a heavy metal door creaked open and slammed shut like the sound of a tractor trailer rear ending another truck. Then footsteps, rubber soled shoes squeaking and stomping like mice and giants. Then there was a high pitched whistle, flipping of switches, and the familiar whirring sound of cell doors sliding open.

Chase heard his own blood pump through his neck into his head. He knew the guards couldn't possibly hear it, but had to wonder as they waited and listened. The footsteps became more pronounced and Chase raised his head to see the outline of two men standing outside their open cell door!

One guard unsheathed his baton and banged on the cage's bars. "Move your asses shitbirds. Now!" He held up his hand for the second guard to stand down and said: "You two stay where you are. Don't move!"

"Fuck you." Chase muttered toward the ground, in that just loud enough to hear something, but not make out the words, and then stood up. "You want to shake us down shake us down dickhead, do what you gotta do."

"Did I hear you correctly?" The guard said, his hand still extended for his partner to remain where he was. "Is that a question asshole or are you giving orders?" The guard took deep breath, raised his arm, and swung his club down hard at an angle striking Chase in the back of his knees. "How's that you fucking crumb?" He stepped back to watch him crumple.

"Mother fucker," Chase had a flash notion of ripping the club from the guard but held back. Gradually he climbed up to steady footing, rubbed his legs and kept himself from making eye contact. "Jerkoff." He said.

The guard buried the club into Chase's gut. "How do you like that shithead?"

"Fuck you." Chase gasped.

He hit him again harder.

Romeo looked on. He hadn't moved, but knew that he'd misdirected the guard. Wearing him out they'd move to the next cell when they regained their presence. Never show weakness or exhaustion a prison guard's rule. Chase did it, he took the beat down and frustrated a search. Yes mon Romeo thought, good job.

"Now get the fuck out of here, it's time on the the yard for you shitheads." The guard was taking shallow breaths, gasping, yet not wanting to show it. His partner stepped into the cell and nudged him out of the cage. He turned to face Chase and the big Black man, and said angrily: "Go on get out. Try not to get shanked out there ladies," he said catching his breath and tucking the baton into his belt. Now he needed a break before he shook down another cell. Dammit, he was too fucking tired to search ANY cell. He had a look on his face Chase would later recall as someone who'd be back. He stood there as the cell door slid shut, looking at the two men with that "accidents can be arranged look" as they shuffled toward the huge metal door leading toward the yard.

SECTION THREE

LETTING ONES GUARD DOWN AMONG FRIENDS

It was a pretty day Milton thought. Looking up he said aloud, "Maybe a three or four on the Beaufort scale, leaves and small twigs in constant motion, look at the flags, they're extended."

"I don't know mon, dust, leaves, loose papers are lifted, and the small tree branches move." Romeo knelt down and felt the grass. "I bet there are whitecaps on the sea."

"Maybe." Milt said. Marveling over the fact that people could smoke again without concern.

The yard was the size of a football field giving the sense of being a gladiator of sorts, surrounded by hordes of adoring fans. However the sensation evaporated with the blank stone walls and razor capped fences maximizing security for the denizens of depravity diddling about on their daily fitness frenzy. Not so much a fanciful feast, but a place where the dregs of society, inmates, who were not innocent could pump iron, smoke dope, or perform ritualistic homicide.

"The guard towers look like sky boxes." Chase said.

"I used to own one at my favorite stadium" Romeo said.

Probably more BS, Chase thought. The inhabiters of the towers were snipers, and there were more than enough of them who would enjoy taking a pot shot at any con remotely resembling a threat.

The Skinheads and Afros were at their respective iron pumping stations. The Lavender Lads, militant homosexuals, snoodled in their zone just not as loudly. The other groups did whatever it is they do, pray, yoga, stand on their heads, or do needle point. Romeo was sipping a chemically laced beverage and commented:

"They say men who get in touch with their feminine side usually have gotten in touch with someone's masculine side."

"I can blow myself." Chase said. "Does that make me..?"

Romeo sprayed fluid from his massive nostrils. He laughed so loud the sound alerted the snipers in the guard towers, and laser beam markers crisscrossed over his heart.

"Shit," he stood up and raised his arms in the usual and customary surrender stance. Finally, after an all clear from one of the guards oh the yard the long-range rifles were lowered, and the guys all along the watchtowers went back to other business.

"Shit." Romeo sat back down and said "Chase don't go be doin' that shit in our cell. I don't like even thinkin' about nothing sexual since my girl left me for my brother. And that pervert stuff...you need a brainscrubbin'."

"I was just kidding." Chase said.

"Focking weirdo." Romeo got back to his discourse on the politics of prison. "The Latinos, they have their own tattoo parlor, and lift weights from first sun till dark. They also got a boxing ring. Now the newbies, look at them," he pointed his chin at the huddles of men in one place or another on the field. "They're fresh to prison, they try to find some familiarity to quell their fears by findin' other folks who did stuff like they did that put them in here."

"Yeah what happens to them?" Buzzing a bit from the booze and puzzling over the extensive knowledge of the African King.

"Usually they end up spending every minute scared shitless, and get the crap beaten out of them a few times. Many of them end up someone's bitch. Others piss someone off without knowing it and get shanked."

"Why?" Chase said.

"Killing practice. Elevates every tribesman a notch or two."

"Why did they stop fucking with me?"

"You got a rep as a major bad motherfucker. I could change that by lettin' folks know about your solo sexuality, but your appreciation of science gets in the way. I haven't had a cellmate with more than a third grade education in some time. Besides, some day you might be of use to me," Romeo said.

After several minutes of watching a minor brawl, Chase asked:"You think there's a way out of here?"

"Maybe." Romeo said. "But we'll talk about it after a few planets line up."

Out of nowhere one of the Nazis approached. Bald, big ugly lightning bolt tattoos, piercings, and all the trappings of a bad-ass wannabe, or maybe was.

"Looks like Question Mark lost his job." Chase said.

"Actually that's his replacement. After you dissed him I think he joined up with the Lavender Lads. Now he's someone's love slave."

"Whatever this shit is it looks like trouble." Chase said.

"That is a version of reality Milton. His appearance, and your memory of people who look like that, are capable of setting off triggers. A series of neuro events which should make you anxious."

"It works." Chase said. "These thugs are going to hurt us or at least try to." Chase said matter-of-factly.

"In India, there is place called the Thugee Pass, where those who pass through it suffer the indignities brought down upon them. A man wiser than myself figured a way to pass without incident. Pay attention. Follow my lead."

"Sure" he said, preparing to die, or at least suffer some bodily harm. "I'll keep that in mind while I bleed out, and make a note to inscribe those words on my tombstone."

"Be Cool. What you're experiencing are externally introduced memories based on things promulgated by entertainment, or some media specific fear mongering. If you can ignore the things you've read or seen, stop and reinterpret them. You can do it. It is then that you will transform your perception. This hairless painted man will appear to be no more than a cartoon of someone, who wants us to believe in our rapid blast of consciousness that he is a threat."

"He still looks like a threat to me. That hidden hand might have a knife. I'm trained to act reflexively, take him out, and get into a fight with his pals. Thanks to the ETOH and slowed reflexes, I'd say I have less than a fifty percent chance of survival."

"Hello guys." Hairless extended his hand in a gesture of goodwill. "Give me five" he said.

Romeo took his hand in his and gave it a squeeze.

The bald mans eyes bulged and his face reddened as Romeo twisted his hand so that his palm rested above the skinhead's, and gave it a few extra firm pumps. Finally stopping, holding his hand and staring him fair in the eye, Romeo let the clench linger.

"This is the Doc, a man of respect." Romeo lowered his chin, still gripping the man's hand. His eyes barreling fiercely from his upper lids. "Do not forget what I say." He let go of the Nazi con's hand.

Bald head wrung his wrist like a Polaroid, grinned falsely, and held his hand out to Chase. "Pleasure to meet you sir," he smiled. He had the mouth of a person, modern dentistry hasn't visited.

Chase didn't appreciate the Swastika tat on his cheek and said, "I'd say the pleasure is mine but it isn't."

"You guys wouldn't happen to have any smokes would you?" His companions approached slowly encircling them, clenched fists over their genitals.

"Only the good Ganja Mon."

The man turned and walked away. Milton sobered quickly. The adrenaline was gone along with his blood sugar leaving him flat. He was thinking about retoxification in a serious way, when suddenly the man turned around.

He said: "Thanks but no thanks. We have to stay pure. By the way Romeo you need anything?"

"What was that all about?" Chase asked.

"Power is in the interpretation of perception," Romeo said as he stood up.

The siren wailed and the time out expired.

SECTION FOUR

WICKED SHOPPING IN NEW YORK

A DEN OF BRIGANDS

In a world where everything is monitored from traffic lights to public parks, getting busted for scratching your balls becomes the reality. You exist on every teleprompter and reveal a face, absent the ski mask, to a world of unwholesome sleuths protecting us from some deadly virulent strain of evil. Fuck it. Go bare adjust your wanger and be another person. It works. All forms of surveillance: face-recog, optic neuropsis, and retroprint of fingers, are already in the waves of the machine. There is no privacy. It's called a public domain, and everyone acknowledges the state of fear in the twenty first century. It's an accepted way of life. You are always surveilled and there is nothing to disavow in the world of necessity you live in. Fear can have an enemy, and that enemy is awareness that a larger system has manipulated you. Failed terror attacks and the military insurance corporate political complex. The goldbricking, ball scratching, slacking enclave of citizens uninsured, without a cause, can be vectored in on and found guilty of one cahoot or another. In some cities there are architectural structures that come to symbolize the limitless possibilities of ambition. Some become the homes for people seeking the ambiance of security, power, and prestige. The mysterious owner of one such soaring glamorous affirmation arrived on a Tuesday with his companion. He was greeted warmly not by the generic doorman, but by a doorman whose broad smile indicated they had a relationship beyond the courteous Christmas tip. Barney Epillito was requested to be at the door "per Mr. Blackstein's orders" when he would be in town. It was prearranged without question that Mr. Epillito would be available. After all, Mr. Blackstein, through a circuitous path of creative financing did indeed own the building. And this doorman assured Mr. B. and company would not have a concern about surveillance on his watch.

The driver opened the door, leaned against the vehicle, and waited until the big guy got out. Looking around he made sure it was all clear and gave a nod to the driver that it was OK to remove the luggage.

"Welcome back to the city Mr. Blackstein," to Barney, the small framed man could have been a dwarf plus or minus a chromosome, he thought. Half pretentiously the other half scared shitless."

The small framed man of indiscernible origin had a penchant for wearing clothing enamored with hearts. Barney, the doorman, couldn't be sure of his sexuality because the very tall Negro, who seemed never to leave his side appeared over protective perhaps a body guard or something like that. Other than the hearts and the Negro the comings and goings of what would appear to be street walking prostitutes, whose chromosomes could be XX or XY didn't really matter.

At "One Sutton Place South" the doorman had the level of confidentiality that your private physician or legal counsel could appreciate. Thanks of course to the fiduciary kindness bestowed upon a simple servant of the truly affluent. Oh yes this little fellow had some oddities, but so did most of the people in the building. Movie stars, reclusive billionaires, the pampered, and pretentious. The man would occasionally rub elbows with them in the lobby. Due to the payments from Jettadiah Blackstein, Barney, could afford that home in the Hamptons and pay for his children's education. He would at some time reflect upon what this chap did to earn his money, but quickly defer speculation because that can get you killed. He did note that the man had an odd nationality, not quite Oriental, and not quite Hispanic, not quite anything he'd ever seen. Jettadiah Blackstein didn't look like any Hebrew he'd seen growing up in the Bronx. Whatever. He had serious loot. After all, the guy's pad in the City was a penthouse with two elipticall shaped parlors and ten foot tall French doors. Barney Epillito, would recall the series of Picassos, Calders, Christ even a Monet. That alone would show up on some database.

No. He didn't live in a more ostentatious place but chose this meager place off Central park overlooking the city like 960 5th avenue, or the Beresford .

People knew the man as Jettadiah Blackstein, an entrepreneur, from the Far East. No one really batted an eye at his affluence as everything was paid off quietly, and then some. When he showed up in New York it was only briefly, and he always left in his limo with one of the sluts he'd bring along after a night out. He used the same limo service, Barney, would recall every time he was in town. For the last few years it was an offbeat company, he did not travel in fancy cars, and tried to keep his profile low. The limo service used beat up vehicles, and the driver with the funny name seemed to be on a first name basis with Jettadiah. His name was Spooky, it could have been a noun, verb, or if the occasion arose, word on the street echoed both.

"Hello Spooky." He had an indiscernible accent and the huge black fellow, bodyguard, lover,who the hell knows? Fuggadaboudit.

The doorman held the door open and watched as he carefully assessed his surroundings. Maybe ex military or something.

Taking his time with the street hooker, "Would you like to come for a ride?" Jet asked.

She was a tall androgynous blonde wigged mini-skirted individual.

"Show me the money big guy, and I'll show you the time of your life."

"Join me on my private little plane" Jet said.

How could she say no? Spitting her chewing gum out.

"You got it honey," she smiled artificially.

The interior of the private hyper jet had that amped up smell like a new car only more intense, and filled with possibilities unimaginable on her usual pittance. If Shoshana"that's what she called herself" could let the other girls know about this score they'd fucking die. So what if the little twerp stuttered. Whatever he wanted would be just fine maybe a little extra too. Shit she'd make more with this guy in a day than than she'd make on the street in a year. She ran her hand over the soft leather seat.

Twenty minutes into the flight and half way through a glass of Cristal the streetwalker's senses began to fade. The peculiar stuttering little man and his tall black friend were staring at her like some sort of specimen, and consciousness slipped away.

A very pleased doorman at Sutton place would be grateful indeed that Mr. Jettadiah Blackstein would be back again, not soon enough. And he'd have another person join him on a trip to wherever. Gotta love the City.

"Hello my pretty." The person being spoken to was on an examination table in a very cold neon environment. He saw her look around. "No dear not the street lights of the city, but my little operation theater."

She tried to move but the restraints tightened with each burst of strength. Her body was being infused with a sedative to keep her conscious as her body's function deteriorated. Allowing her to consciously observe decay, defecate, spasm, and even be disemboweled without even feeling a thing. Jet Black took great joy in watching the eyes of a patient terrified, as their body was being trashed. Damn did he love to see them watch themselves be implanted with cancer, or some other wretched diseases. Ha, what a rush.

Paranoia be damned. He knew what he wanted before having his fun. A good kidney, half a liver, and maybe sewing two left feet on might take the dance from under this urchin's bullshit. Nobody fucks with Jet Black.

"Toodles darling. I love when you watch me work. Yes I did paralyze your vocal chords. I pu pu pu prefer Mozart to moaning."

Piano Concerto #20 in D minor played as he disassembled her body, and put together a mishmosh of dysfunctional organs.

BACK AT THE CELL

"Romeo, I've got a few questions about revitalizing people who've been frozen?" Milt asked.

"What sort of questions?" Romeo replied suspiciously, in that what's it to you tone, signaling it's nobody's business.

"What techno shred does it take to alter the frozen state so that there is certainty the subject reanimates with all systems functional? That shit is by all accounts impossible."

"Why you wanna know mon?"

"Just humor me man. I'm fucking bored shitless and this whole brain scam thing it's fucking cool."

"I look like a focking librarian mon?" Romeo said finally giving in with, sure..."

"Go on" Milton pleaded.

"Criminals came up with it. It would have been impossible if it were not for Pinkus."

"A footnote in history." Romeo stood up and put his hands on his hips, "Pinkus wanted to eat, eat well that is."

"Who is Pinkus? I never read anything about him, or her. Why feed a...Shit is this juniper induced prison psychosis?" Chase shook his head.

"Be cool. This is for real. The Pinkus Pulse is a standard integration of every paradigm requiring a bit more than a sure thing." Romeo usually in repose was particularly animated.

"Before the Govvies of the world busted Arnold Pinkus, he was a graduate student, who had been beaten into a coma by less than savory gaming chaps. He made money scamming casinos in New Las Vegas decades ago. The cat locked in a program that if applied properly..." Romeo said.

"Properly that is from the criminal point of view?"

"You are in jail mon. If you ever get out you're gonna have to make a killing you know. I do not think you'll ever settle for, or be able to accept less. You can't doctor no more, that path got winked out of existence."

"Tell me more about Pinkus." Milt said.

"His device started out stratifying ice crystals. People's dopamine rush came from the game, but there were those who wanted a sure bet. It took some formal presidential pardon for his innovation to be implemented. Of course he couldn't appreciate it. The Pinkus Pulse that is. The PP is standard integration in every tech weapon, or target acquisition device on earth. Its a device used when one is requiring a sure hit."

"Man I was in the Army. I did my weapons training, but had no idea how I managed to fire my sidearm with the accuracy I did. Fucking assholes never told me it was a set up. Unless your bullshitting me."

"Does it look like I'm here on vacation? Sort of a spa ting? You think this world is just as you see it? Things exist outside your high almighty medical license, and fancy cars. The pretty homes with high fences and fancy gates, places maybe you heard about in the movies. The place where I come from mon, it's the street. Everyone lies. You'd have been the perfect mark thinking all the world is like they say it is. It's all a set up."

"So this Pinkus Pulse squirts an electromagnetic reading the colors of cards, or coins, or targets in motion, and is preprogrammed to whatever you want it to be. Jeez the things you learn behind bars.

"So what happened that got you here in this cell?"

"Someone got hurt."

"Always does."

"I screwed up. The Freezare device was fine but the rapid thaw was black market. Very much so mon. Shit from the Continent. The guy I got it from sold me beat equipment, like I got the vibe he knew it'd fuck up. I'd like to freeze that asshole's heart."

"Who was he?" Chase said.

"Some generic chap who wanted some ideas. He gave me the tool and I accepted the funds."

"What was his name?" Chase asked.

"Names can get you killed." Romeo replied.

"I'm in here. The guy that set me up is out there. What am I going to do?" Chase added.

"Whoever set you up is one very bad dude. Personally I'd be trying to figure out a way out of here, and track the bastard down."

"Perhaps there is no way out of here for us. The man who put us here wants us here, and will make sure we stay here." Romeo looked at Chase and shook his head. "At least for now."

"Who is this bad person?"

"Listen to me mon. I know you're in here for murder. Indirectly you killed, or were set up to have killed, a very important financial link to one very bad man."

"I WAS set up."

"No worries mon, most of the chaps here were too. You're as innocent as the next guy. Even the guilty ones are saints compared to what I am going to tell you.

Listen, if you want to know about evil let me tell you a bit you might not have heard in your healing arts world."

"Please." Chase sat with his hands behind his head. An hour before lights out.

"Listen to me. If evil took on some corporeal substantive form, it would no doubt be in the form of one enterprising man and his minions."

"Is this a devil story. Cause with the rest of my productive life behind bars good bedtime stories are comforting."

"Shut yourself up and listen."

"I'm listening."

"This I know is true. Ask around the yard. The worst of the worst serial killers and horrible molesters look like saints compared to the embodiment of the man."

"What man? This is one of those times I wished I smoked."

"I am Romeo Divine-it is my real 'or as real as reality can be' name. I took the name John Grant to hide from this force of nature. I am safer here in prison than I would ever be on the street. Here I can handle myself. Nobody hides from the Devil himself."

"Who is this man?"

Romeo said: "I've never met him. No one has. I have only dealt with his go-betweens."

Chase sat up. "Go on..."

"This very bad dude mon, is an enterprising physician not unlike your very self, but very much your antimatter. You from what I have learned saved soldiers with garbled flesh in the war. You rebuilt broken bones and replaced severed limbs. Some of our fellow guests have even been operated on by you. That's probably why you haven't had much trouble in here. Word is that you're a crazy man."

"That's nice to know. Tell me more about this super bad guy?"

"The demon, I will call him for now, is the owner of all things horrible, and is known among the under gut of crime as an untouchable brilliance, a dim light of darkness. He is an unreachable breeze."

"A ten on the Beaufort scale huh?"

"Mon! Still thinking this is a funny game. A ten would seldom be experienced on land. Trees would be broken, uprooted, and considerable damage would occur, to most structures. The sea would rise with overhanging crests, white, with dense foam, and visibility would be low. A ten ha. This man is way beyond that."

"I'm impressed. You know your wind scales."

"I know people too. You are here for a crime you didn't do."

"Go on," Chase's legs were dangling from the cot and suddenly became still.

Romeo put his hands behind his head and reclined, inhaled deeply, waited a beat, and said: "This demon owns corporations, malls, morgues, crematories, hospitals, and highways. He controls a waste removal operation which globally extricates the forensics of all things detectable."

"How come no one ever busted him?"

"Every grifter, con-man, hired killer, terrorist, and government agency, knows he exists but cannot pin a thing upon him. No one can, or will identify him."

"Why?"

"Anyone who has ever come close, even informers of governments have met death, disappearance, or disease. The man's veil of invisibility and influence is so well constructed that even the families and friends of the one who came close to his putrid eidelon of unwholesome industry simply evaporate. Poof."

"You did business with him didn't you?"

"Look where I am today. Even his intermediaries have never seen him, and the bank deposits are undetectable by ordinary means. His ties and misdirection have elevated him to a place where no one can reach him. That my friend is why you are here."

"You know that?"

"You killed someone who knew someone. A way to trace an obscure wire transfer. A man in Palm Beach. Or so they say."

"The fuck? How could you know that?"

"I know lots of things." King said.

"What exactly did you do John Grant, or Romeo, or whatever your name is? How is it you know all this shit and your still alive? Don't hand me the stealing memory schtick."

"I already told you why. I'm worth more to whoever put me here alive than dead." The lights flickered and suddenly it was dark.

HIGHER EDUCATION BEHIND BARS

For Milton, time tiptoed by, and he dealt with it as a model prisoner. Hardly worth measuring the degree of scams and innovations available to learn, for any willing criminal. Medical school was one thing, but having a solid criminal education, Milton figured, would give him something to fall back on. A month didn't pass without the occasional shanking, and the two cons came to watch each other's backs. Every time the cell was opened for a meal or exercise period the very possible threat of violence kept ones blood pressure elevated. The guards were usually on someone's payroll, and it became obvious to Chase that Romeo had some magical protective shield about him. He always seemed to return to the cell with delicacies, as in pornographic chips that were watchable on the holo player, liquor, chocolate, even tobacco, all prohibited (to other inmates) and lots and lots of reefer.

So there they were, just a couple of cons in the yard talking quantum physics, cranial nerves, and a host of ways how to fill a wallet, warehouse, or get laid on the outside, without paying.

Milton, would later recollect one sunny day in particular, he was just returning to the cell from lunch, reclining on his cot, clearing his mind, readying himself for a nap. He checked his schedule. Nothing too pressing and began that slow path toward an alpha state, and began to doze.

Romeo was already asleep when the usual shouts and shrieks were mere background music in the institution. They'd both gotten used to it the way farm bred folks get used to the sound of cicadas and crickets. What may have been ordinary background noise of a madhouse, was Mozart to the incarcerated, indoctrinated cons and it suited these men just fine.

BANG BANG BANG...The echoes of a stick clanking on the cell's bars sounded like a freight car loaded with percussion instruments flipped on its side waking both men. Their eyes cocked open and they both lay still, waiting to find out what the ruckus was all about.

Finally the voice of a guard cut through the vibrations, "Get up you fucking bums." He banged his beater stick against the bars again. "Move it," he hollered.

"You want both of us mon?"

"Chase, get your sorry ass up!" He motioned for him to come over to cell's sliding door.

"What you got to wake us both up for huh? I'm bleedin' sleepin'. Ain't no manners in this place mon, no manners at all." Romeo said wiping his eyes.

"Shut the fuck up your royal fucking highness." The guard said. "Go back to sleep and dream of the gorillas you'll never fuck again."

"And go fuck yourself too, assmonhole." Romeo fell back into his reverie, and would later recollect this racial invective that needed to be remedied. Not today though.

"Get up Chase," the guard repeated.

"You had me at get up you fucking assholes, boss," Chase looked at an imaginary wristwatch. "What is it, time for a random strip search?"

"Arms out through the bars, you know the drill." The guard, immune to wise cracks, cuffed, shackled, and escorted Chase along the catwalk. Buzzers went off and doors slid open as they walked outside the main cell block. He shoved him with his baton to step up the pace as they made their way across the yard to a separate cluster of small buildings.

"Is this an early release chief?" Chase asked.

"Don't make me have to get physical douchebag," the prison guard snarled.

"Now what?" It was a Beaufort zero day. The air was calm, smoke rose vertically, and there was no motion of the blades of grass. The guard pointed at him and said:

"Don't make a scene or else, you fucking asshole. You got company," the guard cleared his throat, coughed up a bolus of snot and spit on the ground.

"A conjugal visit? I did order a ho."

"Shut the fuck up!" the guard coughed again.

"Gotta cut down on the smokes officer."

"It doesn't look social, so you gotta stay linked up. You know the drill, and don't make me hurt you. I ain't in the mood for it."

"I was really expecting that body cavity check I've had this itch goin' on."

"What the fuck is it you don't get, Chase? Shut up and move, or I'll shove this stick up your ass!" The guard pointed his chin at two other guards looming outside of the small building. Big beefy sadomasochistic looking pricks he would later describe.

"Set up the prisoner for the interview" the crumb boss said, shoving Chase toward the building's door tapping his night stick on his palm. "And take your time too, maybe knock some of that smartass out of him."

One of the beefy guards pushed him through a door into a grey neon lit room toward a metal chair, and cuffed his wrists to the chair's arms, and his legs to the chair's base. "Don't get too comfy asshole." The guard gave him a slap on the shoulder that felt like he'd been kicked by an elephant, and left the room.

Chase shut his eyes maybe catch up on that nap he was on his way to before the screws struck up the band. He didn't know who might be visiting, but figured the only person that would, would have to be his fucking lawyer. Maybe another weak defense strategy that wouldn't work. He still owed him money. Fuck him, he thought. Why pay someone off when you're in jail.

There were two quick perfunctory raps on the door, as if they had to knock, and the door opened

"Come in" Chase said in a sing song voice. Expecting his legal counsel he froze. Startled by the person standing in the door's frame, arms akimbo, tapping a foot.

"Who the fuck are you?"

"Howdy Doc, I'm your new best buddy" the visitor said. He had that Chuck Yeager airline pilot tone. That voice pilots used to keep the passengers calm. "Come to see how you was doin' good buddy." He wore a white cowboy hat. On his blazer was a logo, it was the same as the one on the windshield of the pickup truck. The one that dodged him along A-1-A.

"Not being my lawyer it's a twisted pleasure to see the man who's got me just where he wants me. I didn't get your name?"

"Dillings. As in Special Agent Lloyd Dillings." He shrugged and held out his hands palms up. "I can get you out of here good buddy."

"Just like you put me here. Glad you could spare the time."

"I got the juice to set you free fella," he looked at his watch. Time is all we got sport."

"Special Agent of what?"

"In due time. But for now buddy, we'll just call it a reprieve from these." He reached across the table patted the cuffs and smiled.

Chase looked at the man's smile. Diasthemetic gap and dice cube sized fat teeth. "You got my attention."

"Jailbird boy, you got a lotta time to serve and I can set you free."

"Why set me up in the first place?"

"Aside from taking you down a few notches?"

"Fuck you. Why me?"

"We needed the right man for the job pal. You and that African cellmate are part of a plan."

"Yeah? What plan is that?" Chase said.

"In due time," he said.

"The time is now. You haven't answered my question, so tell me please why me and the King of Africa?"

"Good to see you and the colored fella are getting along. The two of you, thick as thieves. Con man like Grant, his rap sheet is longer than my pecker."

"If you have one. Old guys like you, boners don't come without a pill. Especially with your asshole attitude."

"My life ain't got nothin' to do with you good buddy. Its just fine as wine." The Agent stood up, folded his arms across his chest, leaned forward, and walked about the visiting area shaking his head. He stopped and put his hands flat down on the table. He took a deep breath and suddenly stood erect. "You can stay here in jail or join us."

"Who is the us?"

"The US Government."

"Nice set up Special Agent. What's in it for me?"

"Plenty" he said. Dillings blew air out of his mouth slowly. "That roommate of yours could have killed you if we wanted."

"But I'm here now. Which means you need me breathing."

"That'd be an affirmative good buddy. But things could've gone different."

"But they didn't, did they? Couldn't find some other asshole for your dirty work?"

Dismissing Chase's glib demeanor Dillings continued: "You know you're just one fine asshole. And that jig? He pulled off that Romeo Divine skit so well, her Majesty granted him and his confederates a full scholarship. If he wouldn't have gotten busted doing short cons, London Yard would've never caught on. Oh yeah Doctor Chase, Romeo's quite brilliant, and wants out of here as much as you do. Like I said, you'll get what you want and we'll get what we want."

Chase tried to get up from his chair and slid back saying: "Find another douchbag."

"You're it. And we need one hundred and fifty percent from you, or the next time some jerkoff on the yard wants you to suck his cock you'll end up strangled. And there won't be a guard to do a Heimlich Maneuver. Get it asshole?"

Chase faced the man, "What is it you want me to do to keep me from a cock overdose"

"Catch an assassin."

"Guard!" Chase shouted. "My time is valuable and I've got lots of nothing to do. I guess I'll have to get me some penis floss, or more likely some cauterizer for the dickless scumbags you send my way. Let me the fuck out of here. I ain't doin' shit for you, asshole"

"Come on back good buddy, don't get yourself in a tizzy. We put you through all this cause you are the man for the job. I know all about that girl you were gonna settle on down with. The one in med school who took things into her own hands."

Chase sat motionless and a deep hue of capillary blood flushed over him. "Fuck you! That was a long time ago." Chase said, his eyes rolling into his forehead. "She's been gone for more than a decade."

"No not that one. The other one. Your former fiancee, the gold diggin' hottie. But she blew you off like a fart in the perfume section at Sacks 5th."

"More like an utterance." Chase added. "The scanners's would probably pick up the vapor trail."

"Real funny good buddy, but you can see we know everything about you."

"Give me some details?"

"There's a dead man involved. A powerful broker of some pretty hideous things, who needed to be removed from the board. He was a link in a perverted multi dimensional movement that would've ended your career, and most of the countries, careers, and populations as well. You are the killer elect of one very bad man. That's why you are here good buddy."

"So you kill some bad guy and pin it on some schmuck like me, and the politicos don't know squat?"

"That is the world we live in good buddy," Dillings shrugged. "Absolute deniability works out right fine, don't it?"

"You set me up on a bum rap then come visit to get me to go dark and dirty. And promise me all sorts of goodies."

"You catch on quick good buddy."

"I'm not your good buddy, asshole!"

"You might be after you hear us out" the law man said.

"Yeah prove it. Show me you have some power from high above."

"I do, and I will."

"You really get a kick out of this don't you Dillings?" Chase said.

"You could look at it like that. But hey" he spread his hands, palms to the ceiling. "I do what I do to make the world a safer place, and I do have satisfactions that you couldn't imagine. Besides good buddy, the job's gotta get done and this setup, you in jail for murdering a money laundering chimp, and the African wizard might just do the trick. "Dillings sat down, leaned back, put all ten fingers of his hands together and let out a long breath before making a steeple of his fingers. "The only way to get an arrogant self-absorbed prick like you to come work with us is the way we did it." Chase sat back, crossed his arms and blew air slowly from pursed lips. "Talk to me Special Agent."

"I'll shed a little light. But it sure's hell won't illuminate the room tough guy."

"Listen special agent if I were on the other side of the shackles I'd show you the light, and shove it up your fucking ass. You cocksucker! You set me up and ruined my life."

"You ruined your own life" he replied. "And you done it just fine." The agent looked at his wristwatch then back at Chase.

SECTION FIVE

THE BRUNETTE WITH BLUE EYES

"Doctor." A woman's voice.

"Who wants to know?" Chase asked and looked toward the room's door. A woman with long dark hair and a no-nonsense business suit had entered. She had a briefcase under her arm. He knew the voice and he had a general idea who was connected to it.

The prosecutor's head was lowered and her shoulder length hair fell across her face obscuring somewhat a pair of oddly brilliant blue eyes. Chase recalled that for a moment brief as it was, she looked like she was in her own sort of jail peering out. With one long delicate finger she pulled back a few fallen locks of hair and tucked them neatly behind an ear, and pressed the digit to her temple. The two locked eyes.

"I am truly sorry you're here. It was the only way." Dina Fuentes stood behind Dillings and leaned forward this time making sure her hair was in place.

"Nice to see you haven't lost your pert court room demeanor" Chase said, taking in her cleavage. He knew she'd become self-conscious. He also picked up a vibe that she could sense his tumescence. Maybe he thought prison did that to you the half crazy mind tricks maybe not. She had some nice tits.

"Do you want to get out of here?" She righted herself set the briefcase on the table and crossed her arms over her chest. "Or do you want to spend the best part of your life in a cell?"

"Ah, the queen wears a heavy crown."

"By working with us you will have earned your freedom. Not just a presidential pardon, but the admission that the real killer was captured, and you were indeed falsely accused." She said.

"You're going to get me out of here." He shook his head.

"Yeah right. I want it in writing, and I want a copy sent to my lawyer, and a dozen fucking news venues of my choice."

"Doctor we can do that. She held out a folder look it's all right here." She held out the pardon—a bunch of legal documents—and then smiled falsely. "Now, all you have to do is sign right here," she pointed her chin toward the papers. "Your commission will be restored, but as far as the media..you are not in any position to make demands that are of national security."

"That's right Chase. You and your Negro pal serve us better at what you might be able to do out there than in here." Lloyd Dillings said. "And that ain't nobody's business but ours the U.S. of A." He thumped his chest where a sheriff might have worn a badge. "I'm a convicted felon. Why did this happen the way it did?"

"Sometimes the planets just line up," she said. "You are a doctor with military training and your cell mate is a biochemical genius with ties to an entity that can change the world in ways that would make atomic chaos look like some abysmal stench in the wind."

"What would that be on the Beaufort scale?" Chase asked.

"About a twelve to the tenth good buddy. We need you to come work for us boy scout." Lloyd said. "That Negro con man's already signed up. We don't have anyone as capable as him not just technically but he can get into places we as in the law, can't."

"John Grant AKA Romeo Divine is a snitch?"

"Actually in his line of work conning people 'bad people' that is out of their money is more of the inside man. Getting himself out of jail with you in tow makes him a pretty bright guy." Dina said.

"Making you the roper Special Agent Fuentes." Chase said.

"He wants out just as well as you do." She said.

"Your lawyer is in the next room. Sit down talk it over with him. The documents he'll tell you are all in order. All you have to do is join us, good buddy."

"The catch, what is it?" Chase said.

"Ain't no catch pal. You served your country you know what its like to be in harms way." Lloyd said.

"How much harm?"

"I ought right disclose this up front. A whole helluva lot that includes torture and other sordid little things. But you'll have a good ole time savin' the world."

"What's in it for me?"

"Freedom" she said. "And probably a suitable stipend enabling you to live out your life in whatever way you wish." Dina Fuentes said.

"Or good buddy like the lady will tell you a few decades in this place could make a real impact on you. Who knows? Ten years from now it might start looking like home."

"I take it the leash will be short," Chase said.

"Very." She said. Lloyd exclaimed: "Seems like somebody on the dark continent found a way to knock people off, and steal their thoughts memories and ideas. Statesmen, politicos, terrorists, and even dead folks."

"He steals dead people's memories?" Chase asked.

"He steals whatever's gonna serve him best, good buddy, but that ain't important to us now. What's critical to you and to us is workin' out an arrangement that he has to keep a global network of physicians who can do his dirty work."

"Like what?" Chase said.

"Shit like placing diseased organs into healthy bodies, killing folks slowly who have no one to protect them other than me and Ms. Fuentes."

"Mr. Dillings," the woman cleared her throat. "We are not exactly in the same department and I'd prefer to speak for myself."

"Yeah real beauties like you Dillings." Chase said.

"I'm just doin' my job, convict. You want out of here or not?"

"Go on, tell me more?" Chase said.

"We got some leads on this guy and know he's out shopping for something. Not sure exactly what yet, but you two are the perfect pair to get in on his operation and find out."

"You still haven't answered my question. Why me and Romeo?"

"Because you good buddy got the bona fides. Hell why wouldn't some bad sumbitch trust a couple of convicts. This is the job you and the King of Africa were born for."

"There are several million perfectly good schmucks in here and out there who'd have a lark playing spy games."

"But you good doctor are more inclined to save lives than see them wither." Lloyd said. "Especially your own. The fact that you can't be frozen is one helluva way into a world where memories are mined."

"How'd you know that?"

"That Juniper juice has some kind of way of stopping the freeze. From what I understand you got so much soaked up gin it'd take an ice age to reach even half your brain cells." Dillings said.

"Amnesty, immunity, and a new life, is there for the taking," Dina said. "All you have to do is stay drunk or aerosolized or on a strict diet of Worcestershire laden food."

"I don't need a presidential pardon for that."

"Listen good buddy its not so much you, but the two of you are worth more than you are individually for this project. A Gestalt of sorts. See the Rastaman has the street credo and more connections than a crooked Mexican nuke plant. He got the smarts to get you in the door and do his thing-ma-jig, and you have the skills to take it down."

"Just what is the it?"

"Like I said we just aren't sure yet, but we have a few leads."

"Like I said record cleared and exoneration. I must tell you that JohnGrant was in on this from day one." Dina bit down on her lower lip. "Immunity and a nice stipend can work wonders."

"Both of you criminalized boys can be out in an hour." Lloyd said. Chase rolled a few thoughts around before giving up anything. He could appreciate the medical device. It was used to suspend the valence electrons of the carbon atom. It had been used in the underbelly of things to suspend life and steal thoughts. Romeo AKA John Grant was no thug. Chase was aware of his breadth and depth of knowledge and knew that by tweaking Heisenberg's uncertainty principle: a concept brought to life theoretically whereby the physicist said that merely looking at an electron circling an atom would change it. You couldn't change the carbon atom unless it was stabilized. That's the glitch. Cryonics wouldn't work ten years ago because you couldn't rapid freeze and rapid thaw. Times change and like the planets around the sun a change in orbit would turn the oceans of earth inside out. This guy was the real deal and he might be a ticket out of this shit hole.

"Listen special agent even though it sounds great I need some quality time with my lawyer. This is all pretty weird and I want to see for myself if this is Kosher."

"Go right ahead good buddy," Dillings said crossing his outstretched legs ankle over ankle and blowing air through those very thick teeth. "I'm pretty sure you'll see things a might more clearly after that little ole chat."

It was less than twenty minutes before Chase sat in front of Lloyd Dillings again.

"Surprised it took that long." Lloyd was looking at his watch. "I don't particularly like lingering about this dismal prison. Ya'll know what I mean?"

Chase shook his head: "I don't much like it either, and this place," Milt looked around the room "It's reserved mostly for law men like you to interrogate guys like me, or set up some sort of deal. No Special Agent Dillings it's not the friendliest zone for the incarcerated."

"Did you make up your mind good buddy?"

"I suppose we'll go out through the back door?"

"Pal we got your six," the agent said. "Yep, we got your good old tush. Just don't fuck it up!"

SECTION SIX

ALLS FAIR AIRFARE

The plane ride was choppy. An old Gulfstream 55 with worn leather seats and frayed carpeting. John Grant tapped the window. "So we're following the money. The Caymans are a nice first stop. My good friend Myron likes to call himself Myrone I worked with him in the past. Very inside job sort of man. Pulls off the African English Barrister maneuver quite well. We studied at Oxford together."

"You never said you went to Oxford?" Chase said. "Bull fucking shit. Was that Oxford Arkansas, or Ohio? And I sang on a gondola in Venice." Chase added.

"Actually Oxford's answer to the gondola is the Punt. It my friend is a flat bottomed boat that is propelled with a pole. Punting on the Cherwell and the Isis is a time honored endeavor."

"That's what the locals call the Thames." Dina said.

"That's because Oxford's Bridge of Sighs links Hertford College and New Quads."

"Very well put Special Agent. In the background one can see the semicircular Sheldonian Theatre. Quite the diversion. As for my name—John Grant no, not in England. Romeo Divine AKA <u>ME</u> the King of Africa is entitled to some leeway in an otherwise cruel and heartless world."

"I still can't fathom you conning your way into Oxford." Chase said.

"Believe me there's a long checkered history of the African King, and his High Street goings on with his pal Myrone Candella. These guys actually conned their way into staying at Blenheim Palace, one of the stateliest of England's baroque homes."

"How do you know all this?" Chase said.

"We know everything. So gents how do you want to approach this?" Dina said.

"We know that Dr. Black owns hospitals and clinics around the world. He gets his financing through a system of derivatives. He has covered himself with so many layers of deceit that nobody can truly find him." Romeo said.

"But he needs a go between," Chase said. "Is that right Romeo?"

"That boys and girl is who we will meet with his liaison for the Russians. Major revenue mon. Don't forget in some circles he's a legit person. A money making humanitarian they say. Ya know he got nominated for a Nobel Prize? Jeez, mon. Three more miracles and he'd be a double saint. Street has it he actually nominated himself for the Nobel prize."

"Nice touch for a serial killing saint." Chase said.

"He's given memories to those with nothing to think of but suicide and darkness. People with nothing to do but play out notions of blowing themselves up along with bunches of innocents."

"I don't think there are any innocents." Chase said.

Romeo continued: "Implanted thoughts of those he's conjured, stolen and shoved in. His patients come from around the world."

"Maybe outer space too." Chase said glibly holding up a glass of gin.

"Who could know?" Dina said.

"Shit. So I have to go to work for him to find out don't I?"

"That there's the general idea good buddy." Lloyd poured him a shot of gin.

"Don't you see Chase you already have the street credential. You are a convicted felon and Dr. Black always needs good criminal surgeons." The woman said.

"As if there aren't enough?" Chase said. "I know at least a dozen orthopedic surgeons who'd put in a black market knee joint or just poke a hole and put it up."

"The fact is that Myrone is on the books for some serious crooks. His old pal Romeo AKA John Grant will get you into door number two all the quicker." Lloyd said.

Chase stared at Dillings.

"The guy you killed," Lloyd held up two fingers of each hand making quotation marks and winked. "Let's just call him the dead guy for now. He was some sheik of sorts. That rascal had some very close ties to someone your gonna be doin' biz with."

"Shit." Chase thought. He would rather play cards with Dina Fuentes in that not so serious way.

Dillings walked away.

"She is a hot little number in that—you know...the sweeter the meat the closer to bone sort of way." Romeo muttered in that inaudibly naughty and sly way reserved for men who know about these sorts of things. "But she's trouble mon. No damn good." He drummed his long dark fingers on the arm rest.

"I heard that, Romeo. You speak as if you've got some serious expertise in that area too." Chase pointed his chin at Fuentes. "Women that is, broads."

"Listen Milton, that little prosecutor is not just a baby sitter. She may look like a ho, but she is a Fed. And the last time I looked we are still crooks on the books. Get with it! They put the ionized mesenteric Locatox chips in us—that should've been enough. They gonna really set us free? Think about it. We do a job they put us back. Maybe even kill us. Think about it?"

"Locatox chips. I remember we used them in the service. Implanted GPS which go biologics—integrate into the brain—vis-a-vis undetectable if captured. IF captured—Boom you're in a body bag! They said they'd remove them to dummy you up so you wouldn't get tracked by the bad guys after the black ops guys took them out."

"You believed that?"

"Why not, I had a medical commission. What did I give a shit. I didn't join up because I had an exactly pure past, and really didn't give a shit. Besides the implants were absorbed through the gut, I figured nature would pass it out of me in a few years."

"Hard to get rid of mon. I wager most of the patients you treated were soldiers back then. Still walk around tracked like criminals cause of the psy-ops of war, and fucked up in their heads. Stupid Americans."

"Cool it with the stupid American shit already."

"Please." Romeo said. "You are what they want you to be."

"I don't have to worry about that. I know I'm not a criminal. Can we order more beverages on this flight?"

"I guess so Mon," Romeo looked around the plane.

"I'm not a fucking criminal asshole." Milton said again.

Lloyd and Dina seemed to have gone into repose for the remainder of the flight. "But you always will be a criminal. Signed, sealed, and convicted. When you forget that you lose track of what could accidentally, purposefully, happen to you. You think you can flush that crap out of someone's body, do you?"

"Yeah, I do," Chase said indignantly.

"Of course you can. A child could do it if they paid attention to basic physics. Between you and me I don't worry 'bout a ting. Once the little birdies the molecules sitting on receptor sites get a blast of alkalinity over a Ph of 9 the shit gets eaten up."

"That's all? Why not just die of old age? That will tear your guts apart and then some."

"Well it is a rather MAJOR shift in pH. Like the alkalinity to the point of death."

"Sodium bicarb to the max?"

"And then some." He smiled. "Done under cryo."

"That could kill you. Besides I've never been frozen. Have you?" Chase said.

"Yeah. Its cool. You zone out and come back feeling a little bigger cause the ice expands things somewhat. You need say a half size bigger shoe."

"Is that a body wide global enlargement? You know," looking down at his crotch.

"Yes mon. But getting back to Dr. Black listen, we can do this and get free, and even better, get rich. Think about it all the more reason to gain access to Dr. Black's team. Ta tell you the truth this whole trip can either fuck up our lives, or make us rich. To me its worth the chance. I see it as a challenge, and jail or death are the only options. You will be frozen and brought back to rid yourself of whatever they implanted in us. Its the only way. But you have to lay off the Juniper for two weeks. Shit just inhale pure ETOH fume for a buzz."

"The Juniper has kept me in a liquid state for so long. Knowing it interferes with the ice trajectory pathways it would be tough to let my guard down. Besides it'd be a bigger stretch to trust you when I'm frozen. After all

Romeo, you roped me in on this in the first place. Shit you might steal some cortex."

"There ain't a big market for being drunk and stupid."

"Fuck you." An air host arrived with a tray of little bottles of liquor, some lagniappes, and ice.
Chase pounded down two minis and sat back.

"Steal cortex off of your Caucasoid gin-soaked mind? Impossible. But you are right Milton, I would not be big on the trust situation with myself either."

"Thanks."

"But if we're gonna get outta this...You gotta make lemonade from lemons. Maybe if you let me, when I'm doing a scan I can jig away some memories making you drink yourself into stupid land. But you gotta jettison Juniper."

"I'd rather have Gin out of water," Chase's voice was thick. "Remember the Duppies of the Old Virgin Islands in the Caribbean?"

"Ghosts. Restless spirits of the dead. The Duppies, according to Island lore live at the roots of cotton and Bamboo trees. Big Juju mon. Oh yes my friend of these things I do know indeed. We all have our ghosts."

"Well, I've got too many. Shit it'd be a cortical genocide for me," Milt became still, dug his fingers into the armrest, "I'm gettin' real tired we'll talk about this later." Chase said.

"That's exactly what I mean Milton. It already is later."

He spoke to a largely intoxicated surgeon about to enter a world of retched dreams and memories, unknown fantasies and grim realizations.

Chase was slowly falling away into that irritable sleep, watching the clouds beneath them when suddenly his central nervous system exploded with an over-sensory change in cabin pressure, and burst into an awareness. He shot up in his seat sniffed and tried to stand up. It was a smell or an audibly imperceptible sound that stirred him.

"What's going on?" Good training does that. He looked to his side, fully functional cranial nerves intact. The abducens nerve, the sixth cranial nerve, arises from its nucleus beneath the fourth ventricle in the pons, and supplies motor fibers to the lateral rectus muscle of the eye.

Prolonged intracranial pressure accompanying high altitude makes the well trained soldier's unconscious kick in. He shot a sideward glance. No matter what state you're in, this one's reflexive. The first step in assessing a situation as benign or hazardous. Sensory nerve hyperactivity was an essential on the battlefield.

The first cranial nerve, relaying smell, could at times be overwhelming and tampering it to ones need was a process which made shit stink worse and pheromones of fear detectable within greater distances. Then again there were those pheromones of sexuality that Milton honed to a highly pleasurable level. And the eighth cranial nerve, heightened even the slightest sounds, so that he could hear an ant crawl when on high alert.

After his first few days of prison through the here and now he was on full alert, and all systems potentiated each other in a symphony of a heightened neuroenergetic state. The sideward glance the smell and sound all fit together arousing a cascade of biochemical events adding up to a steep physical attraction.

There she was, standing next to them: "My ear receptor picks up everything you guys say all I have to do is listen for it. And with my bioframe," she pointed to her left eye and grinned mercilessly at the miscreants she had to baby-sit. There was a small freckle Milton would later recall it was on her face, probably an interlocutionary elemental tag—all I have to do is cross my eyes—which she did, to see and hear you. And boys you don't ever shut the hell up. Damn. I can pretty much see everything you see, so stop staring at my ass and focus on the mission." Dina Fuentes clenched her fists and dug them in at her hips. "Remember most of your cranial nerves are monitored by me and the rest of the team 24-7. Listen hard and remember: You can earn your freedom or return to your cell. Try not screwing it up. The alcohol is on board because this plane is used by congress not convicts. Don't abuse it."

The plane hit some turbulence forcefully throwing the woman off balance. Despite her best attempt she fell on to Chase's lap. The two men looked at each other. She would later keep in mind the crafty smirk John Grant had on his face.

"Most of the cranial nerves?"

"Some for the obvious reasons had no use. The first one, olfactory sensations are things I can do without."

"For a prosecutor one year out of law school you do have a chunk of tech and a trough of tough. What really is your back story?" Milt asked.

"Enough to know that a law degree would protect me from doing things to people I'd like to without spending my life behind bars. Besides it was part of the Agency requirements."

"You didn't quite say what agency that was." The King of Africa said.

The plane stabilized. She stood up righted herself and said. "No, I didn't, but here you are a couple of free birds."

"Mon I like that," John Grant drummed a reggae beat `Endless bird you cannot change, free bird I can't chay ee aye ee aye ange, free bird..."

"Are you finished Rastacon?" She said adjusting a bra strap.

Chase said: "Hey he's just adding levity to an increasingly tangled mess we've entered. I'm not the sort of person that sits well with the last period of time I've been through. And let me tell you bright eyes, I'm still not sure if your boss if that is who Mr. Lloyd Dillings says he is won't try to zap my memory of this and toss me back in the slam."

She crossed here eyes. "Listen we know King Con of the Jungle is the sort of people that gives that sort of people a bad name. You're too soaked in Juniper to even offer you a blanket. When we make a deal we keep it. If we didn't there'd be no one to do business with."

She went back to her seat looking at the image of the way Chase looked, looking at her. Prick saw me blush. Gladly pleased she couldn't smell their farts. Elimination of the first cranial nerve sensor was at least to her as she would later recall, a wise choice. Especially when monitoring the felons in her charge. Self consciously she looked at her champagne glass filling breasts. Quite comfortable with herself. Chase lamented: "I haven't been with a woman since my fiancé realized there wouldn't be a wedding. She canceled the registries and decided visiting me in jail beyond her child bearing years wasn't on her agenda." Smart girl Dina thought, monitoring their chat.

"Fock her mon. There's gonna be some things gonna make you smile and they ain't part of some plan you think you're part of."

"She heard that. Fuentes that is."

"Good." The man in the Dashiki smiled a mouthful of dice cube size teeth and sipped on his Cognac. "I want her to know I love private jets and my choice of wardrobe."

"Sort of rings of that King of Africa thing. I need a few Ethiopian's tossing rose petals before each step but I don't think the government will spring for it."

"It'd be a nice touch." Milt said. Holding his hand up for another beverage which would never show up. "If you want to get the part you have to look the part."

"You didn't leave prison without an education Milton."

"We got the part." Milt settled back and stared at the sea below.

SECTION SEVEN

ON LAND

Grand Cayman was a flat island with little or no redeeming value as a bargain vacation. The untold trillions of dollars legally passed in and out its banks and financial institutes daily. The population, mostly barristers, bankers and bean counters developed the tiny piece of earth into a haven of sorts for folks with stashed away funds, hidden from the prying eyes of the rest of the world. The scuba divers snorkelers and sunbathers after all knew that the overpriced little island housed their stashed away funds. The plane was losing altitude fast and hard as the short runway made for a near arrhythmic rush until the jet's tires screeched to a halt. Chase would always remember thinking that the island needed some augmentation, and likened it to flat chested woman.

Under the cover of very bright equatorial daylight (the kind that hurts your skin when you're out in it) they were greeted by a nonchalant driver seemingly bored with the things he'd been doing. Newspaper in one hand and a sign in the other. It said: HERE IS YOUR RIDE.

Spooky Pollack, or that's what the driver's tag said drove slowly through town pointing out the alleys and crevices where someone if need be could maneuver oneself from an uncomfortable situation, and arrive at their destination unseen. "I will be at your service 23-6."

"Don't you mean 24-7?" Chase said.

"I mean what I said." He looked at the three passengers and shook his head. Leaving Chase to wonder whose side this guy was on.

The condo on the touristy empty Seven Mile beach was a three bedroom up and down unit that allowed each of them a reasonable degree of privacy. Chase opted to take a swim after dumping his luggage. Dina said: "Don't get lost."

"I wasn't planning on swimming to Cuba." He put on his mask and snorkel and paused. "Unless of course you care to join me Dina. It'll take the stress down a notch."

The frisson was obvious to Romeo. But romance could interfere with the grift.

"I didn't bring a bathing suit." She looked at her watch. Mr. Grant will be setting up our meetings hopefully we'll get something done today."

"Hey tough little lady down here my name is Romeo Divine, Dr. Romeo Divine PhD. Remember that well because you are going to be Milton's personal assistant, and he is going to be opening a bank account."

"I'm glad you're on board Romeo. What a name." She was setting up her work desk. A three dimensional holo platform and computer the size of a dollar bill and several square coins. "Romeo we know you were born in Detroit relocated to Jamaica in your teens, and weaseled your way into a full scholarship in England."

"So we do little lady." Romeo said. "I like to travel."

"Asshole. I am not anyone's or ever will be anyone's Little Lady!"

"Not even for an hour?" Chase said.

"Dr. Chase," she said. "Whatever money you use is ours, as in the agency."

"We've been through this too many times and now that we're here winging things is the only way this is gonna work," Romeo took authority. "We are now on MY turf and if this is gonna get done it's gonna be my way. I don't care how tight a leash I'm on."

Chase was wondering who the intended victim of this planned con was. He learned that a short con means taking the mark for all the money they have and it ain't pre-planned. It didn't seem his cell mate was going for a quick score from some government agency. Romeo was a long con player. He knew more complex trajectories—planned maneuvers—whereby the mark, or marks are sent to get more money or whatever. Oh yeah, this was gonna be a big con and Romeo was putting her on the send. Putting in the fix was con artist slang for cooperation with the authorities and those like Dina with political connections can get you places. And this banker? Who was that going to be? The US Federal government or this mythical bad guy?

The King of Africa said: "Listen I have to work an old friend for information. That's going to be difficult and it will take some funds. If you want to get the part you got to look the part. Like I promised I can get us in the door and you and your puppeteers are going to pay the price for a job well done. There can be no tension, at least no detectable tension between us. My old school chum Myrone is by his nature a very suspicious man. He cannot see me as an ancient escaped convict. He can get a fix on things very quickly. There've never been any beefs with Myrone."

"I'll be sure to wear my thong panties."

"Listen Dina if I tell you to wear a miniskirt and spike heels to get something done and you refuse you will have compromised this little maneuver. You will have wasted a lot of time and money and the bad guys will get what they want. You will be an out side man—woman. You identify with the mark and gain his confidence. To Myrone you will convince him that you are Milton's personal assistant even if it means full throttle fellatio in the men's room to prove you're on the team." She looked at Chase's blushed flesh. Chase slid down his mask and scooped up his swim fins. This was going to be curious.

"That I can fake."

"Well fake it good if you have to."

"I've got a few skirts and lots of shoes in my luggage. So go get yourself prepped or whatever it is you have to do while your buddy over there goes sightseeing on the reef."

"The last thing we want is for Myrone to believe he's excluded from a piece of something. Especially when I show up in full Afro regalia. Myroney goes to the authorities over here and its over. He's an old friend, but has lots to lose and might take a bit of convincing."

"Chase knows about this?" She asked.

"We spent long enough in lock up to know what a play off the wall is. Using a con in a real setting not a hotel room but his very respectable office has its obstacles. There will be a need for backup and he has to be comfortable with it."

"Please?" She said."A weapon." Chase said.

"Something I'm familiar with."

"Unloaded." She said.

"Perfect." Romeo said.

The car pulled up to take them to the law office. The driver shook hands with Romeo/JohnGrant/King of Africa. No one noticed the tiny shred of paper that passed between the handshake. The wink in the rear view mirror acknowledged that the driver could side with the obvious winner of a good scam. Good old Spooky. Romeo shook his head and smiled.

"What's so funny?" Milt asked.

"This is gonna get good my brother. Real good."

"What are you two babbling about?" Dina said.

"Stupid prison shit." Chase said.

Spooky Pollack drove them from the beach condo to the financial capitol of the criminalized world.

Here was a building filled with discrete offices offering little or no indication as to who they belonged to. The office building was located in a district surrounded by several other similar hurricane resistant structures. This small island housed the wealth of most of the uncivilized criminal world. Then again the politicos preferred the Isle of Man especially after the Panamanian fuck up and the New Swiss Ordinances.

"Let's do it, folks," Romeo said donning a beret. "We gonna make the earth move."

Myrone Candella LLB was a Solicitor (England and Wales) with the G.S. and Whitney Corporation on Grand Cayman. Quite the magistrate would find his filings favorable, and his education not so dissimilar than that of his former roommate at Oxford Romeo Divine. Romeo's passion for the hard sciences made Myrone remarkably curious as to how the world of physics and bioscience would eventually change the world. Ah but a pair of not quite Caucasoid brothers native to Mother Africa found an abundance of comfort in that they were selected from among the upper levels of society. They gained entry into a world of dirty little secrets (as well as big dark ones) of colored acquaintances and a host of quirky individuals with connections from Gstaad to Malibu, and every place of wealth in between. A treasure trove of mutually respected colleagues. Many who could and would be used to manipulate variables otherwise unavailable to those members outside of an elite campus life in London.

"Mr. Candella is looking forward to seeing you." The Oriental secretary in the five story building had a keloid on her chest. Chase would later recall as pretty gross and wondered why she didn't have it removed. Then again there is that subset of people who wear their moles warts and scars like some twisted badge or medal. Largely things which would stimulate only one thing the 9th cranial nerve,-the gag reflex.

Dina had on her mini and the look on her face melted when the secretary held up her palm. "Sorry no women are allowed into the office of our Solicitors." Romeo introduced the Caucasian: "This is my very good friend Milton. He's cool to the point where he can come and meet my old school chum. He is to be a customer of the firm you should know."

"Of course Dr. Divine. Coffee, Tea, or..." The barrister said jovially, but in the serious guarded manner those occupying positions maintain, "or. beer?"

"I'll take a gin and tonic," Chase said.

"What a freaking office you have Myroney Pony. I thought you'd be selling pencils in Mayfair."

"Shut up you fucking Lloyd pain in the ass." They embraced, Myrone's legal wig was on his desk and the gown looked like serious business. "NSY hasn't even smelled a thing" Romeo said. "I go underground change names a few times and you, you stick with the one you've stolen from a cemetery all those years ago." Myrone looked at Chase and his skin spoke in a darker hue than words.

"Don't worry, he's cool. So am I and I can stay that way forever-you know that." Romeo said.

"This isn't just about opening an account is it?" Myrone sat behind his desk. He pushed the intercom button and told keloid girl to bring him a Scotch.

"He wants to open an account." Romeo took a pen from his desk and wrote a note and slid it to the Lawyer— THE CHICK IN THE LOBBY IS A FED, it said.

Myrone stared at the note, held it up and looked at Chase.

"He's part of the team mon be cool." Romeo winked at Myrone. "Just play it straight and we'll all get well from this." Romeo moved his hand beneath his chin like he was chopping his own head off smiled and said. "Let's talk about it all at dinner."

SECTION ANOMALY

AN ARROGANT EVIL

The man spoke softy: "I am glad you have come to my clinic Dr. Lowell." Black said. "You young woman are one of the chosen few who have come to this place."

Indirectly yet somehow right to the point he spoke as if she might not have existed but for him, allowing her to be there. She stared at the little man and thought judging by his insouciant demeanor, his lofty tone she'd heard before. Pseudo superstars and laureates of considerable and dubious achievement use similar tones. As if they were rock stars who've saved the earth. Smarm. Pure unfettered little man compensatory hoity-toity babble. The woman seated across the immense desk knew he was going to be a prick, but not this over-the-top. Who the fuck is this guy Goldfinger?

"I'm glad to be here Doctor." She said.

Maryellen Lowell MD saw a semi-oriental man an admixture of some odd genetic expression. He was of an indistinguishable age, but had a presence which however old he was made him seem ancient. He sat with his eyes shut and looked like he had just finished smelling a dirty diaper.

"Have you any questions dearie?" The man said.

"Are you prepared for experiences you have perhaps only had in your dreams? Nightmares te-he-he, that is."

A small smirk appeared on his face that looked she thought, like he'd just lit a cat's tail on fire.

Where the hell is this guy coming from the woman doctor thought, as she stared at the man with a heart badge on his lapel.

The man seated behind the granite desk placed his palms together. They were positioned as if in some meditation, or perhaps what could be perceived as prayer. He knew she was at this place of last resort for something to do to pay her bills.

"Perhaps little darling you have come to the correct place."

She said nothing, nothing at all. Lowell crossed her ankles, her knees pressed firmly together. She felt a storm well up inside but remained cool and waited before responding.

Several beats passed and a tension hung between them like mayonnaise on a raw burger. Foreign and foul.

Finally the man behind the desk raised his eyelids and stared through her at his ego wall.

His medical diplomas looked like they came from some of the finest highly regarded schools in the world. But they didn't. Something was off but what? Maryellen couldn't tell for sure, but she knew that there were two R's in Harvard. She needed a job and this was her last shot before serving Slurpees at some mini-mart. There was a giant aquarium to her left his right, filled with the weirdest looking specimens she'd ever seen. In fact they were deformed. Some of them two headed fish-ugh. What the hell she said to herself, what's few freaky fish and phony letters. She tried to focus on the positives which were few other than the money.

"You like fish?" He pressed something somewhere and a wall panel slid upward revealing shelves of specimen jars. "Maybe you will find this fascinating dearie."

She tossed her head back lowered her lids and closed her eyes for a moment considering what would come next. Finally she pressed a finger on her temple and opened them to take a look

"The sea gives us many beautiful things," he pointed his chin toward the aquarium and shifted it to the shelves with an abrupt notch of his head and continued: "But the real magnificence of our knowledge is here," There were containers on the shelves of human organs in various stages of decay. "You like these don't you dearie?" he asked not expecting a reply and continued, "Someday I may show you my real trophies."

"Are those human?" She said trailing off. What a twisted fuck this guy was.

"Doctor it is truly sad that you cannot practice Plastic Surgery in the world because of...shall we say a few little problems you seem to have had' Hmm..."

She drew her eyebrows together and cringed: "We all have problems."

"Of course we do dearie, and we all have redemptive qua qua qualities... But your skill set is special. I am just beginning to appreciate these things. With your problems precluding you from what you can do...Perhaps you just may have come to the right place."

"Dr. Black," She leaned forward letting her hair brush the sides of her face and waited a few beats.

Slowly she raised her head took an index finger from each hand and tucked her stray locks behind her ears. She said softly with dispassion: "Those were not my mistakes or my problems just errors that could happen to anyone."

"As they never are dearie, as they never are. But those errors DID happen under your supervision didn't they, dearie?"

She shrugged shook her head and bit down on both upper and lower lips. Should she tell this freak to shove it?

"Go on, look at the organs sweetheart," pleased with himself. "They are quite amazing."

She reluctantly left her Eames chair righted herself and walked awkwardly toward the containers on the shelves. After a few moments of study she held a hand up to her mouth. "Holy shit these really are human aren't they?" Referring to the lungs, hearts, livers, and spleens, in large glass jars.

He feigned insouciance but inwardly chuckled and pretended to review her documents.

"Modifications. That is wh, wh, what I like to call them," he said referring to his organ collection. "You do have some wonderful credentials dearie," he let his gaze drift toward her buttocks. "Very nice indeed."

"My bona fides are right there sir. But the organ collection, I don't get it?"

"All preserved on the sub atomic level and perfectly capable of restoration and implantation."

"Why, or how?"

"The fish you see are mutants. Preserved in the acidity and alkalinity of the sea. The ocean itself is the formalin of today," he smiled wickedly.

She sat back down and looked at him. Sick fucking ass hole she thought shaking her head slowly. "You implant diseased organs into normal human beings, am I getting this right?"

"Of course. Someone has to. These are disease free only chromosomally manipulated to alter at any given time. A time of my choice, that is. Does this sound interesting to you Doctor?"

She shut her eyes and chewed on her lower lip. This could be her last shot at doctoring.

A very full lip at that too Jet was thinking. "We also have an array of artificial joints and such packed with the latest explosives. A wonderful weapon quite costly as well."

"And you expect that I would be performing those procedures?"

"You are looking for work dearie. Aren't you?"

"Yes but this is mad. And you expect me to do these things?"

"Why else would I bring you here? Does doing the work many would die for frighten you? Do you think it is somehow depraved?"

She wanted to tell him but who knew what this man was capable of, and how far would he let her go on knowing? She was trapped and knew that she'd just crossed some line and her moral compass had a whole new North.

"Listen up my good doctor. There are wars and there are warriors, and there are fortunes to be made from the attitudes of the little people who persist in destruction. I am simply an arbiter of the true horror we can willfully induce. Showing the enemies of the enemies what can be done makes me not a mad man, but an envoy who may some day bring a quiet peace to a world with false hope, distorted information, and flat out lies. Yes I can cure, but killing and the threat of a knowledge of ones own demise works wonders on influential charlatans."

She didn't move. Legs tightly crossed,"I have nowhere else to go. But if you can restore my license after this I think I can do the work. Just one thing, I don't want to know who or what the patient will do or die for after I've done the procedures."

"Okay dearie. Now tell me please how do I know I can truly trust you to work with us?" He said.

"You don't. But I am a well trained surgeon and 'my problems' as you call them, you say you can resolve. I'll owe you for that won't I?"

"We shall see," he raised his eyebrows stood up and walked slowly around his desk and smiled. "We certainly will see dearie," he placed a hand on her knee and smiled. His teeth were perfect.

She felt an urge to vomit but somehow held it back, and faked a nod and grin of acquiescence.

He took his hand off her leg jolted to attention and hollered, "Simmons!"

"Simmons? what's going on?"

"You'll see dearie. SIMMONS where the fuck are you?"

She exploded uncontrollably into a visceral panic. Sweat poured from her body. "Who's Simmons?" Choking back tears.

The man came into the room held out a Freezare and turned her to ice.

"Thank you Simmons. We will review her memories and see if she is suitable. If not bring her back with some very life threatening illness. I'm partial to a metastatic breast cancer for this little cold fish."

BACK ON GRAND CAYMAN

"Okay Myrone where does he get the money to run his operation?" Romeo said.

"I'd be in breach of my legal obligations."

"Listen mon you have more to lose than a public hanging. Word gets out of our way into school could be kind of life altering thing. Don't you think?"

Myrone said nothing. He just stared at the diplomas on the wall.

Romeo continued: "Some things in your world could raise more than an eyebrow. Growing up in London as an orphan street hustler. Your application to Oxford was based on MY legitimacy."

"That was some time ago. Many years have passed." Myrone said.

"Shut yourself up Myrone. Romeo Divine King of Africa. Shit mon, you knew I was playing the JohnGrant from Jamaica from day one. When you wanted me to help you pull a short con on an old widow I turned you on to a life. A life I must remind you that you would never have had."

"The King of Africa," Myrone's tone waxed reminiscent. He lowered his head and slowly began to grin. "That was quite innovative, old mate, quite rich indeed." Myrone wore a wide smile.

Romeo knew it wasn't fake. He saw the tiny wrinkles between the eyebrow and lids you can't fake that, no. He stared at his old con mate fair in the eyes and continued: "Nonetheless I can prove my personal history without a reasonable doubt. You Myrone very well know it to be the truth. Even a lie a believable one must be grounded in truth."

"Excuse me for interrupting," Chase barged into the dialogue and stated firmly, "How the fuck did you pull that shit off Romeo?"

Romeo shook his head slowly from side to side, took a deep breath in 'the as if I actually have to explain this manner' and said: "Mon, I had to go into hiding after my parents were killed in Africa. The provisional government back then did not want a trace of monarchy. I was sent off to the States then the Islands. I had a new name. Sure they tried to find me—destroy a lost legacy—but I disappeared. I was somebody else's dreg on society for quite some time. Happened to have been long enough because the political climate of the Dark Continent changed again and became part of The Larger Europe. The lost legacy resurfaced with his trusted genealogical records and his trusted friend and we both gained entry into that wonderful palace of Academia where St. Fridside the patron saint of Oxford founded the abbey where Oxford's Christ Church stands even today."

"It's true. Shit," Chase muttered.

"The most salient parts of any tale always must be. I hope you're satisfied? Now lets get on with what's at hand," Romeo said.

"Okay okay we'll work something out. It'll be between us," Myrone said.

Chase, sitting to his left, said nothing. He just watched them chatter and looked at the shelves of files in the office wondering how many contained deep dirty secrets about crooks, smugglers and other international outlaws. Maybe even a fallen despot or two.

Myrone seemed to be doing something beneath his barrister robe something most people would consider odd, but when he whipped out a Freezare and zapped Romeo into a block of ice that thought, on Romeo's part was frozen.

"What the fuck?" Chase was on his feet and had the weapon wrenched form the barrister's hand so fast that Myrone couldn't let the air out of his lungs he'd filled before freezing his pal. Then again the Ranger choke hold Major Milton Chase had on him would've made that moot if Myrone didn't come clean fast.

"What the fuck was that all about?" Chase hollered, ready to finish off the island lawyer with another squeeze to the throat.

"Relax man. Romeo wanted me to do this," Myrone could barely speak. His hands were in the `I surrender' position and his eyes bugged out like they'd fly out of his head across the room if Chase didn't ease up.

"What is this about, Myrone? You trying to fuck with us?"

"No. Not at all I had to do this. Romeo's orders. Let me go so I can finish this up or he'll be damaged. I have to bring him right back."

Chase let his hand go loose. "You're going to thaw him out?" He stepped back and looked at the robed man. "Are you saying this was planned?"

"Yes," Myrone rubbed his neck. "Romeo let me know he was coming-and made the arrangements. See this," he held up the weapon. "US Government issue, Romeo had it delivered. Now stay clear and let me get on with business."

"You know what needs to be done Myrone. We're on the same team right-?" Chase continued,"If you don't I'll kill you" He looked at his frozen cell mate patted the frozen flesh of his shoulder. "Cold motherfucker. Cold."

"This could be a real mess you know. Especially if it doesn't go well" Myrone said, "If he fails to come back you know, as he was…" his voice trailed off, then he blurted out: "Now step you're white ass back and shut up and let me do my job. We ARE on the same focking team old boy the WINNING team!"

"Okay, okay," Chase held out his palms. "You better be right, asshole" Chase said indignantly.

"Trust me we'll all be grateful when I bring him back." Myrone said.

"You can you do that…Here, now?

"Of course," Myrone looked at his desk, motioned to Chase in the `is it all right for me to do this manner' got the OK from Milton and slid open a drawer. He held up another odd, at least to Milton, looking device. "Can I do my job now Doc?"

"You better know what you're doing. What the fuck is that thing?"

"He'll be just fine when I bring him back." Myrone had walked around to the frozen Negro.

Myrone had studied this procedure with his pal a Rapidthaw device in his hands.

"It is a Rapidthaw it warms without warming but keeps the electron orbital as stable as the moment the subject is frozen. It is comprised of a flash UV spectrum of light to bring him back a subject."

"Back to what?" Chase said.

"Back Milton to someone without those little surveillance implants little miss Dina Fuentes and Lloyd Dilling's can toy with."

"And I can't have mine taken out because I'm saturated in Juniper Juice," Chase added. "I know I can't be frozen because of it. Romeo said he'd take care of it at the right time."

"Well, this isn't the right time," Myrone said, and proceeded to thaw out the King of Africa.

AT THE BAD GUY'S LAIR

"Simmons it appears our funds have had some intrusion. Accounts frozen and others missing or diverted. Especially after the fellow in Palm Beach you know the so-called Sheik Abdul El Kazar was killed. It seems that since he was dispatched the government of the United States has been a bit intrusive."

"Who is it that squashed that little insect I allowed to handle my South East American interests?"

"Milton Chase MD, Orthopedic Surgeon." Simmons said.

"Why did he do it?"

"Word is he's a drunk and went crazy."

"What became of him?"

"Went to some TMZ167 prison for murder." Simmons said.

"I do believe that phony sheik was filling his pockets with more than his due. I like this Chase fellow a good mechanic is hard to find. He does have the criminal potential. Is there any way we can arrange a meeting?"

"Too late. Word on the strasse is he's out of jail. I don't know how but the brother he was in the cell with, Romeo Divine had a phony holo pad in the cell."

"Romeo?"

"Not only do I know him but his work is legendary. His Rapidthaw and Mempack operations would be an incredible asset."

"What do you want me to do?" Simmons asked.

"Find them you ninny. It would make things work brilliantly. These men are perfect for our operations. Both of them. These men would serve us well repopulating a fucking world of terror."

"They could be with the Feds?"

"They don't send their own into a prison. Especially a TMZ and certainly couple him up with that African King."

"I'd watch them carefully if we do locate them. I want to know what they are up to. If its suitable we lure them in. Make them think they've come to us."

"Yes boss. I'll get on it."

SECTION EIGHT

Three Hours Later

"The new girl has been processed," Simmons said softly bowing his head.

"Wonderful Simmons. Please send her in and make her feel as if this is the last place on earth she would visit and the first place she would come to for help."

"Can I play with her tits when they warm up?"

"Shut up you imbecile. We are not having any unnecessary exams here, not today." He paused and put his index finger beneath his chin. "You know Simmons since you have been so good at your research I will make an exception today. Go, feel free to take whatever liberties you wish," knowing there wasn't much harm he could do to his specimen. "Then you can thaw her."

"Thank you Dr. Black."

ON THE FLAT LANDS OF THE CARIBBEAN

Milton and Myrone watched Romeo slowly reanimate. He moved Chase would later recall, like the Tin Man from the old Wizard of Oz when he first got oiled in the forest.

"That's really somethin' that quick thaw Myrone un-fucking believable."

"Yes yes it is," the Barrister nodded.

"So Myrone, where does Jet Black get his moola?" Chase asked.

"You're kidding aren't you? Even acknowledging this chat you know could get me removed as a legitimate solicitor."

"You're not legit. Never was never will be." Romeo now wringing his hands, "Damn it's been a while since I've been frozen. Go on tell him..."

"That's not the point Romeo, I need this job..."

"You need to breathe too mon," Romeo said as if he'd not been a block of ice just moments earlier.

"Not telling me can get you killed." Chase said.

"Stop being childish Myrone tell the man."

"Telling you anything will get me worse than killed." Myrone looked over his shoulder he was sweating in the frigid neon office. "I've got a few deals going that involve some very dangerous clients. This whole thing with you Romeo and Dr. Chase has caught me off guard, you wouldn't believe what I went though to get this far. These guys will be here soon. Shit. I shouldn't have even mentioned THAT." He sat back down.

"Look," Chase said holding up his Colt 45. (Dina allowed the ancient weapon sans the ammo for the leverage Chase thought he'd need) "Myrone you're as good as dead any way. Romeo and I are convicted felons and have about as much to lose as your pubic hair. Shooting you would probably be fun. Starting at the knees."

"How did you get THAT past the metal detectors?"

"Schmuck I used a metal deflector." Chase held up a wallet sized device and cocked the gun.

Myrone stared down the barrel. "Shit I just disengaged Romeo's Locatox tracking chips. That was the deal. Tell him Romeo." he looked toward his old friend.

Romeo put out his hand, "Chase lower the gun."

Chase obliged. "You've come this far with us maybe we can help you with your uh difficulties..." he was breathing heavily.

Romeo said: "Calm down Milton. Let me deal with this. Listen up my very good friend Myrone, we want to divert large quantities of the mysterious mister to another wallet. Sort of flush him out. You are entitled to a piece of the action."

"What action?" Myrone said.

"Good stuff Myroney." Romeo looked around the rather over the top elaborate office. "But not cooperating might bring some. You have nothing to lose by joining us."

"Its been a nice ride." Myrone Candella looked at the white haired wig on his desk. "I do what some messenger says. Yes I am familiar with portions of his bleeding books, and I do represent concerned interests. Certainly you realize I am just a cog in a very complex set of gears which can easily be sawed off."

"Myrone do you know how many people he's killed, maimed, and ruined?"

"It is not my business blokes. I don't know him but he haunts me like a bad allergy. Always a little reminder." Myrone said. "I know this position I'm in can make me rich but I am afraid."

"We all die." Chase said. "Why not live well and help us put an end to this creep?"

Myrone pushed back his chair and stood up. He ran a hand through his curly hair. "I do not know which way to go...But this is what I do know: He always needs new doctors, and his funds always zig zagging wherever he wants. Always to some crazy place or another. He has the Russians running in circles searching for frozen remains, and pays for the bodies with good clean money."

"Money that I know you wash for him, no?" the King of Africa said and paced about the office shaking his head from side to side. Finally he said: "There have been more than some Eastern Block characters visiting our little island. It's their business they say. Lots of it too. They say they own him. The US and Brits have frozen some accounts, but there is so much more."

"It will be your business to find it. When you do you will reinvent yourself again. Or perhaps my old friend, not even bother. You will be rich beyond your dreams with the blessings of the US government. When my man Milton and that little Sheeba take him down that money will not go into someone else's harmonious home, not some government agency. It will be ours!"

"Listen to him good." Milton said threateningly. "Can you think of a better way to get well than stealing from a shit bird who'd just as soon cut your dick off?"

Romeo chimed in: "That little girl out there," he notched his head toward the waiting area, "would just as soon put us back in the slam. Probably figure a way to take you down with us, but you'll help us get into Jet Black's life and divert that money because you can and will. Not much of a convincer to think of your own charitable direction."

"Mon Chase you learned well in prison."

"Continuing criminal education thanks to the US government's lay away," Chase said softly and shrugged. Then brought up his tone a few notches to the holler level aimed toward the waiting room: "You catch that honey?" knowing Dina Fuentes was monitoring their conversation. Less than ten seconds later she was standing in the doorway. She had one hand on the doorway's frame the other balled up and resting on a cocked hip. "Listen Chase you're on MY time," this isn't a stinking party." Her tone was professional albeit edgy with a touch of feminine angst. Chase would later describe it as pithy.

She said: "You've already implied complicity in a criminal enterprise Myrone. Do you really want to go further with this?" Dina Fuentes walked into the room and was standing in front of the barrister's desk.

"How did you get past my secretary?" Myrone began to stand up.

Dina "I popped her in the head with a bitch slap to the bone before she could press any warning buzzer or security switch," she said with a confidence tone.

Myrone sat back down and pursed his lips.

"So there are a couple ways to play this Myroney," Romeo said. "One, you live with wealth and an eye over your shoulder and die quickly. Or, like one of Dr. Black's minions with some kind of cancer or an implant of sorts that takes you out slowly and painfully."

"There isn't much to think about Myrone," Chase said. "One way or another you're fucked the bad guys are going to own you, or the Feds 'as in the lady' are going to set you up for a trip to Guantanamo."

"I thought they closed that place?" Romeo said as he locked eyes with Dina Fuentes. The room went still. No one spoke for a long moment and a tension hung in the air. The only sounds any of them heard was the large clock on the wall ticking off seconds, and the grinding of Myrone's teeth.

The Afro Cayman barrister took a few more quick glances over his shoulders and finally let out a long whistle through his teeth. His eyes bulged when he said:

"Okay, okay, I get it." Myrone held a finger to his lips, shook his head, took a pad and pen from his pocket, scribbled a note quickly and handed it to Romeo, and folded his arms across his chest.

It said: "The room is bugged meet elsewhere."

The King of Africa looked at his old pal nodded and passed the note for Dina and Chase to look at before reaching for the pen and pad scribbling a few words for all to see. "Take meeting to beach."

Myrone knew the deal. If you were part of Jet Black's team you lived in fear of some wild and whacked out punishment at any given moment. Shit, bursting aneurysms or slow growing tumors whatever it was-Jet B. owned you.

Myrone didn't have another way out. This was legit whatever it was. An offer from a US Fed and an old pal was better than a life in fear.

They would meet in two hours. He'd already been monitored by the security system A system the Eastern Blockbusters would forward to the Man, Jet Black. He already had said and done too much today to take back or explain to either Jet or the Russians. Myrone knew at this point there was no turning back. It was just a matter of time till his own time came, and Myrone wasn't ready for a premature death.

CUTTING A DEAL ON THE BEACH

Myrone gazed out at the sea as they walked along an isolated stretch of Seven Mile Beach. Finally he shifted his gaze toward land and studied the terrain. Finally they were away from the row of condos, hotels, and beachgoers. He was satisfied the group hadn't been followed and directed his stare to his friend the King of Africa: "Romeo, I have been thinking about things." He glanced over at Milton and the woman and continued in a high tinny voice: "Listen people you are not gonna walk in on this deal so easily, it's dangerous, and I am the one taking all the risk."

"So what are you doing trying to weasel out on us and go back to your little law office prance around with that wig and cape and wait around until someone bumps you off?" Chase said.

"No. I want my cut up front." He said firmly and stopped walking. Folding his arms across his chest he pressed his lips tightly together and looked at Chase, Dina, and finally locked eyes with Romeo.

"Consider it done Myroney. Have I ever let you down? All you have to do is make things go as we wish."

"More than I can bother to count." The barrister smirked and let out a lungful of tense breath. "Give me some specifics and I'll get things in motion."

"I want to enter his world," Chase said. "I want the intermediary, the spook, the go between, whoever it is and I want street cred. I want to get a job working for Jet Black."

"Why may I ask would you want this?" Myrone asked.

"On account that going back to my life the way it was 'my private practice in the US' isn't an option for me anymore." Chase said. gruffly.

"We'll all be dead if this fails. I can't go back into the bank at least not after today. No, never again. I will be a marked man."

"Not if we do it in a way that will make everyone happy." Romeo said as the group strolled slowly along the shoreline.

Dina chimed in: "I think there are a few ways to work this. But first Dr. Chase will have to enter the lion's den. From my knowledge Dr. Black has a marvelous way of retaining his employees.

When his funding is discovered to be gone he will at first suspect some government, as the US has frozen many of them and modify his benefactor's transmission."

"Your CIA NSA or whatever did a precise albeit illegal maneuver finding my firm to be involved in funding and dispensation. However Romeo and Milton," Myrone began to say. "Look no further than the street, Spooky."

"But he has to come to us first. Finding him through misdirecting assets is a start." Dina said. She was wearing the bathing suit she said she didn't have. "It'll raise an eyebrow with the Eastern Block hoods they'll want blood and shut down, or at least make things difficult for his acquisition department. Especially when they find out he's ripping them off."

"Let him know that there are forces you cannot control but that there are other avenues of wealth to work with." Fuentes said.

Myrone said: "I'll come in with you along with total immunity, new ID, and of course, my cut."

"Your cut," the woman said with a neutral tone of disapproval. "You want?"

"The money," he replied. "Of course."

"Of course," she said. "Now spew..." it was an order not a request.

"This very evil man has something in his possession something he bought from the Russians. It is quite valuable. So much so that it strikes horror into the hearts of even the most desperate criminals. I am not so sure what it is but can only tell you it is something he can reanimate, and with it they say control the world."

"Myroney," Romeo said. "Who's they?"

"You know who they are, the street mon."

"Can you give this guy an out?" Chase asked Fuentes.

"In the US yes."

"Okay. I'm washed up here anyway. Its a big world madam," Myrone dolefully said. "I'll let the Russian know that his money isn't getting to its destinations. Then we conduct a little maneuver of our own."

"By the way Myroney where's the best place for us to insert ourselves into his organization?"

"Miami, Florida."

"Book a suite. We'll need to set things in motion." Romeo raised his head. "Make it somewhere central and someplace very very nice. It is after all, on Miss Fuentes expense account right?"

"Do I look like your fucking secretary," Fuentes said.

"After that prison retreat it's the least you could do," Chase added.

"Fine," she said defiantly and exited to make the arrangements.

SECTION NINE

BACK AT THE LAIR
Frigid Impulse Career Moves

The frozen woman Maryellen Lowell was nude. She was seated in a wheelchair moments from being thawed.

Dr. Jet Black looked at his man Simmons and smiled. "So pretty she is. Motionless and every cyclic nucleotide awaits our immersion into her deepest neuroelectric pathways." He ran a finger along her leg. "Take her to the lab carefully, this one I might not want to lose."

"Sir?" Simmons asked.

"Go on, warm her Simmons, she'll do just fine in our Djibouti center," the small statured man shrugged.

Simmons would notice the shrug and identify it as a sign that his boss might just want to have sex with her.

"Put a capper in, make sure she can't utter a word of her meeting with me. The laryngeal carcinoma activator goes well with those who decide to get chatty. Oh yes, and alter the motor neuron disease gene to activate the pseudo bulbar atrophy. Make sure she knows it too. Constant crying always throws one off. Oh yes, modify her fifth and seventh cranial nerves so chewing and tasting become somewhat of a task. Maybe a recollection of child abuse, yes, at sixteen by her uncle. Insert greed and remove conscience. Give her a good chip of hatred for all humanity." Simmons was nodding. "Yes sir. Very nice touch. It works for me. What if she doesn't have an uncle."

"Make one up," Black said. You're a big boy.

Simmons was a very big man. Perhaps six ten and held loyalty above life. After all Dr. Black had implanted an aneurysm in his brain that could rupture at any given press of a button. He knew that too, thus making for a serious somber guy who would likely die for his employer. His residency was cut short by a very unseemly sexual encounter with a dead patient. Cardiothoracic surgery had no place for a giant pervert with a fondness for the dead. His penis was in the right atrium of one very warm corpse. Dr. Black loved his taste in organs. His penis was incredibly tiny for such a huge man. Nothing that could not be fixed. However Simmons fondness for the cadaver could not be altered and his master provided an abundance of warm cardiac tissues. Two hours later Dr. Jet Black knew just about everything in any way that Maryellen Lowell had impacted in her cerebral cortex. She was not a threat. No transponding devices, a real history of illegal activity and a penchant for mind altering substances. There was a troublesome pathway indicating that she was aware of Dr. Black's mythic history. He smiled inwardly. She knew he killed his parents and froze them with what might have been the first Freezare. But nothing sinister. She was a complete fuck up without a job, and likely facing jail time. Even mythological mogul's need a concubine.

Maryellen Lowell was appointed as a new physician in the chain of hospitals and clinics owned and funded by Dr. JB. As the head of plastic surgery her daily chores of cosmetic and reconstructive procedures to the poor stretched on longer than the memories she had lost.

BANK ROBBERY

It was roughly four in the morning give or take a minute or two when the bank was robbed. The simplicity of it lay in the hands of one very well educated and highly motivated soon to be invisible solicitor. He did have the scan card and keys to the law offices, and the pass codes and transponding caps to deflate the economies of several countries. And it was all done with a few taps on the keypad. The next day of course the warrant for his arrest was issued and the furious bad guys of the world ready to shred his ears did not matter because Myrone evaporated. Courtesy of Lloyd Dillings "R.I.P. team" he was on a private flight to wherever he wanted to be with a whole lot of money to do with what he wished. Or so he thought.

PISSED OFF RUSKY

Anatolie Sarkov had little reason to suspect the funds he was about to transfer from one account to another would evaporate, and then be revived in some other place. He found out about the account on the Isle of Man. Funds had been transferred without his approval.

That certainly got Jet Black's attention. Big shot master criminal being ripped off by a hack lawyer in the Cayman Islands. Being happy was not Sarkov's job.

Finding and killing Myrone would be simple, but getting the money would not. Sarkov's favorite customer, Black, was going off the books.

Ordinarily a dead man, or soon to be a dead man would dare steal from us. Sarkov considered the options. He could use the lawyer Candella to make more money and get back some of the delicacies he provided that fucking mutant Jet Black over the years. It was a lower upper level decision by the mobsters to put him to work if and when they found him, and then strike him down. But before any of this he had to find him. After all this is not the American Way.

SECTION TEN

YASMINE AND SPOOKY

Yasmine worked New British Columbia like a maestro conducts Mozart. Sticks to the mind for a few hours and leaves a sour longing for the concerto for days on end. A pseudo hooker as in she didn't really sell sex but; it was a steady income stream of high priced flesh non-holo games routines. A tantalizing short con. Maybe what Milt would call a seven on the Beaufort scale with whole trees moving in the wind. Resistance felt walking against that force of nature. Oh yeah. She could make the sea heap up at near gale force and white foam streaks came off the breakers. Her MO, as Romeo would describe was quite of an elegant and entertaining woman. She shacked up at the Four Seasons. Rooming in a suite with Bobby Culture, a truly short con operator and made the rounds. The spa hotel and its indoor/outdoor pool made for an easy spotting point for the wealthy. The marks across the street at the Hong Kong Shanghai Bank and the Vancouver stock exchange were easy pickings. Nab some schmo on his lunch hour and bring him home while Bobby picked his ID. Money was moved as well as personas, and embarrassed Johns didn't give much a shit about it. There were not going to be a lot of married guys saying: "Hi honey I just got ripped off from a hooker and lost all our credit chips." The only box anyone could expect Yasmine to present "in one way or another" had to have a Cartier or Tiffany ribbon on it.

Whoever it was the Russian Mob, US Intelligence, British MI5, it didn't matter. Whatever or whoever paid the highest price for information, he'd take it. A man who'd sell his balls for the right price. Spooky Pollack. The rogues rogue. This week he was the driver for Jet Black and his man friend, bodyguard, whatever. They had done business in the past because Spooky had a good reputation for having a bad memory. He parked the car after dropping Simmons and Jet Black at the door.

At the Four Seasons bar approximately three minutes later Spooky walked into the very drab room and in an unconventional manner sat down. He was hunched over and his palms were uniformly moist. His heart rate somewhat elevated and he had sense of some dark dense cloud surrounding him. He would describe his state of mind as moderately grim with a chance of frightening.

Spooky had several portions on his limited platter. Things which very well could make him very ill, in fact if played poorly very dead.

The fact that he immediately recognized an old acquaintance as they did too was frightening. The man was Bobby Culture and the woman Yasmine had mutual knowledge of many other of those hovering about the periphery of the many semi-legal actions which lined their pockets. Yasmine was a big girl with a big heart and healthy appetite. Whatever it is they would be working on wasn't going to work too well today. He made a quick about-face and went back to the car to think about just how rotten things could turn out. Spooky being who he was happened to be quite pleased that no one in the bar paid him any mind. Bobby Culture was a bass guitarist in Jamaica when Romeo Divine, then known as JohnGrant, plied their skills with a going nowhere fast band. All the members of the Reggae ensemble including Yasmine and Spooky himself shared a similar disgust for any nine to five way of life. The mutual ideology made for a splendid relationship.

These days Yasmine was a bit more elegant than a mini skirted urchin. She liked to think of herself as an actress with the role of an expensive sex expert. The long legged pose with a strategic tear in her stocking, the heels, the glimpse of lingerie through her blouse. Many gentlemen found her attractive in that naughty sort of way. Not quite slutty but maybe not unwilling for a romp of sorts, and most certainly would offer to buy the woman at the bar a drink. Among other things she did love a good Manhattan and an array of ways to tantalize the mark, including but not limited to her ability to tie a knot with the stem of a cocktail cherry with her tongue. Nonetheless the Streetwalker, the Johns, and the hotel room with a built in thug as in Bobby Culture to roll (or play the spurned lover) ensured that the bills would get paid.

Primitive as it was one evening, sitting at the Vancouver Four Seasons bar she chanced upon a potential mark. It was the big guy standing in a bodyguard sort of periphery that sparked the hairs on the back of her very lithe neck that made her consider taking the day off. Jet Black spotted her and she spotted him.

Jet was on a shopping trip and the woman looked compelling. She didn't think that her pimp, a gentleman she referred to as her chaperone, could handle the immense bodyguard and opted for a small time chat before excusing herself. But the big guy's hand on her arm went unseen to the bar's patrons and the wad of cash left on the counter made Jet Black get up and walk to the car alone. Simmons and the girl would be joining him soon.

But something happened. Bobby Culture noticed the hand on his girl's upper arm and followed them out the door. She was freaked.

Spooky Pollack did not acknowledge his old acquaintances and sat in the vehicle contemplating what his next move would be. He watched Yasmine and Simmons come out the door. Shit, Spooky thought. Knowing them would implicate him and put old Spooky in a very bad position. Jet Black had just taken his place in the car, sat back and waited for Simmons and his girl of the day.

They both watched her pimp follow the woman out the door. Bobby Culture grabbed her other arm and said: "What you think you doing?" Simmons was trying to pull her away from Bobby Culture.

"This looks like trouble, bossman?" Spooky said, starting the engine.

Jet knew for sure it could be trouble. Especially when he noticed the pimp Bobby Culture. He would later learn that he was unwilling to let the woman go and Simmons was on it. The pimp was in his face, getting too close and too loud, and the woman's fear evoked a burst of perspiration making Simmons loosen his grip.

"You're not taking my girl?" Bobby hollered. "I am Bobby Culture a respected citizen, and this man is trying to steal my woman!"

Simmons let her go just long enough so she'd have little play, like a fish on a hook, then grabbed her by the hair. "Nobody tells me what to do asshole."

"Honk the horn Spooky. Yell for Simmons to get his ass back to the car. Quickly!"

"The fuck?" Simmons knew the deal wasn't going to go down.

She pressed the palm of her hand down on his and he let go of her hair. She wriggled away from him only to stare at the two men on the street. He looked at her with the sort of menace only a clear and present death could punctuate, and she took a step or two back.

She was trouble a definite no go. But the pimp...he isn't going to ruin my day. Simmons throttled the former bass guitarist in such a manner that every neuron in his body lit up before he died. Yasmine ran to the fallen pimp and screamed bloody murder as she cradled Bobby's fallen head.

It took her a moment but she looked about and the whole scene crystallized in her mind. It was the driver, she had known him from somewhere. Someone from her past. Shit.

"We gotta get out of here Fast!" Jet said.

Simmons dove into the open door of the car and they sped off.

Jet would have to find another specimen but not in this town. The hooker could pick Simmons out of any line-up and Jet did not like that. He also did not like knowing that someone could be close enough to have seen him.

Jet spat on the floor of the vehicle. "We can't just kill her. Too many people will recall our faces, and the tracers even in this hoser country are everywhere. Facial and Cranial Nerve emission transmissions are tracked so well we could be killed on sight. Shit the girl has to evaporate. Can you farm this out Spooky?"

"I think it be a good move you be leaving Canada for a while bossman. Broad like that ain't gonna go away and hide."

"Yes." Jet said reflectively.

"Broad like that probably turn up dead anyway. Especially without her pimp. Best us not being around when she does."

"Spooky, Spooky, Spooky, always pragmatic." Jet said. And pressed the button that raised the separator between the front and back seats of the vehicle. Spooky was not privy to his confidences with Simmons. Of course Spooky recorded everything. Simmons said nothing but Jet Black smelled an envy which disturbed him: "Simmons if you want to go back and kill her do it. But it had better be clean. That was a lot of body to dispose of."

"I could do the girl clean." Simmons said.

"But why bother. In a day she won't recall a thing. She'll be too busy mourning her pimp and drugging herself to a world nobody would believe." Jet said.

Spooky rapped on the window between him and the passenger compartment. Jet lowered it down a bit.

"We're home," Spooky said as he pulled into the alcove at the Four Seasons.

Jet forgot to roll up the sound screen and was unaware that Spooky, always in favor of his own best interests overheard the colloquy: "Simmons, have Spooky ready the plane. I think I might be in the mood for Mexican tomorrow some spice. You know? A bit of screaming."

Simmons said: "Things are heating up. It's getting more difficult maybe someone is on to us. It's starting to become more difficult to do our body shopping."

"Ha difficult? More of the challenge, Simmons."

"Boss it is becoming more difficult. Almost like we or YOU are being watched by someone, or something."

"You're just being paranoid Simmons."

"No. Think about it. All the surveillance everywhere and who knows maybe somewhere someone got missed and you were being sought out..."

"Simmons you mean US."

"Us, boss. Us. I know sir that you love the bodies of the nobodies, but having them come to us has always been the easiest way. Maybe we went out of our usual patterns."

"But finding them ourselves Simmons the hunt and the kill. The harvesting of their organs and their strange and unpredictable memories."

"I understand sir." Simmons said. "But the times have changed. I know you'll miss the adventure, but..." Simmons voice trailed off.

"Ah I will miss the thrill of the kill," Jet said. "I truly love the raw unfettered subject. But you are correct. Too much surveillance and there ARE some rather feisty people who I have come to learn trying to pin something on us. Let's skip Mexico or even Costa Rica. We'll grab a quick slut in Miami, head home and do a few interviews. And I do look forward to viewing our new doctor. I'd like to see her in practice watch her do a few procedures you know. See how she does in the OR. Does it sound sanguine to you my dear friend Simmons?"

"Thank you boss." Simmons rapped on the window noticing it was partially open. Pausing for a moment he wondering if this ignorant driver understood what they were discussing, or banging around some nonsensical music in his head. Whatever just something to keep in mind. "Slow it down Spooky we don't need a routine traffic stop. Not tonight." Simmons said.

"Gotcha, bossman," Spooky said. Simmons thought that this peanut Negro driver without but a degree on a thermometer is manipulating my patron to put me in a bad place. I am Dr. Simmons to you.

Simmons whose career move of sexual anomalous fusillades, and issues with tissues did not at all want to be overshadowed, or lose his job. Spooky Pollack and his dimwitted point of view was not going to second guess or get in the way of anything. Perhaps an accident for Spooky can be arranged somewhere down the road.

"Simmons. You know the power I have and I sense some dissatisfaction. Let it pass-it is not worthy of you to consider."

"Yes, sir." Simmons said.

"Simmons, we must find ourselves a fist to shove up the ass of those who want to destroy us."

"Colorful boss."

Jet twisted his mouth in a way that Simmons would later recall as someone receiving some very retched news about their gonads.

When the facial spasm ended he said: "Fuck the US Feds when we get to them which I know we will, you can have the pleasure of destroying them. You will appreciate the fiduciary advantages of your position will you not?"

"Thank you sir." Simmons let out the foul deep breath he'd sucked in. Spooky just another bimmy. There are some bigger fish to filet. Damn that Jet Black, the fucker could read his mind. Or perhaps it was the bioereceptive chip on his aberrant wanger that Jet Black could monitor from any number of neurostim implants he had looking after his operation.

Spooky quite purposefully overheard a rather enlightening conversation and began having some minor anal leakage. He held open the door at the Four Seasons smiling as he bowed. He was indeed talented in monitoring his employers whereabouts and recording his activities. It was in that just-in-case sort of way if he had to produce some documentation to save his ass. "I'll have you at the airport minutes after you call." He knew that Jet Black's finances were somehow restricted. His usual accounts had begun asking for collateralization for purchases. They wanted to see some of his alleged substantive assets.

Too many questions by too many people were one thing. But when it came to fueling the private jet an old contact who usually worked on a revolving credit wanted gold bullion. For reasons unbeknownst Jet Black's bank account numbers seemed to have been manipulated by someone who might just be powerful enough to cause some damage.

Maybe Spooky thought he might not be working for the right side. After all he did have friends in low places, and maybe this was the time to get in touch with them. The throttling of Bobby Culture. What if he was really fucked up, what if he was dead. Shit. That did not sit well at all with Harold Spooky Pollack.

Spooky had come to know many things through his sources. Among those things were the names of people who could either make your life on the street decent or miserable. He knew people you never, as in ever, crossed. One of those men was Romeo Divine AKA JohnGrant, whatever suited him at the time, but, for the most part he was known as the heir to the African Throne. And word on the street was that he had been liberated from prison. The King might be just the man to reach out to.

Maybe he thought reconnecting with Romeo Divine might not be a bad idea. After all they had done some maneuvers in the past, and the King was always a proven winner until of course he got sent to the joint. Jet Black was too fucked up with his hooker shopping and crazy twisted ways. With Bobby laying on the sidewalk shit, who knows? Someone else he knew could get fucked up. Yasmine might have ridden that ticket and ended up on the other side of daylight. Maybe, Spooky thought its time to get away from this crap grabbing turd.

SECTION ELEVEN

Spooky's Golden Dreams

When the time came Spooky and Romeo hooked up and this is what went down.

They spoke on a secure line. Harold Spooky Pollack told the King of Africa: "Simmons the guy working for Jet Black gave Bobby a rough time."

"I don't know for sure, but he sailed into him hard, so hard he probably had to go to the hospital. And then I thought he'd beat Yasmine too. It's not a cool gig anymore."

"Tell me more," Romeo said. His voice tense.

"We were hangin' at the suite, the one Jet Black owns at the Four Seasons Vancouver. Man that guy's got pads all over. I know some bad shit is going down for him. This is what's happened: a few months ago I found out about the gold. You know that I can size up a piece of luggage from the old airport scams. Those bags the 'Vuitton shoulder's' can hold maybe what forty fifty pounds? This big Mandingo nigger's got me schlepping him over to the bank for a couple days in a row. He'd take in a few empty Louis Vuitton shoulder bags and come out with them bursting. That goon Simmons, made me unload the bags and schlepp them up to the suite. Shit. Old Spooky ain't no dummy I could hear the metal bars clanking around so I take a peek in there motherfucker! Big ass gold bars. I ask myself how much did this guy have socked away? I knew about Jet's briefcase filled with Baer Bonds I checked that out when he was taking a crap. I still don't understand how they work. But I do understand gold."

"Go on Spooky,"Romeo said.

Spooky continued to tell Romeo about Vancouver

"Room service had just left when Simmons opens up this huge Louis Vuitton trunk. Like I said all those trips back and forth from the vault. I probably shouldn't have been in the room but these guys were seriously distracted. It was that big coated canvas trunk with the iron banding and black lacquered metal corners and wood lathes that spells serious money to me. This one was different because it was filled with gold bars." Romeo didn't respond for a few minutes. Finally, "Go on Spooky."

"I know this is a lot but listen, I was figurin' each bar must weigh what 26, 27 pounds and these guys are working like maniacs filling a couple of these trunks that I end up schlepping to the airport. That Simmons was laughing at me trying to load those fuckers onto the luggage carts. I said fuck you to the asshole. I know how to remove things from airports, but getting them in is a whole different story. This Jet Black has some very powerful connections."

"What kind of connections?"

"Damn this is some heavy shit. Mostly he works with the Russians they keep him invisible. They sold him the G-55 with stealth capabilities as well as all the fake ID he'd ever need, and a bunch of other goodies. His credit used to be good with them even though I already paid for the fuel in gold. This Sarkov guy some sort of boss was waiting at the plane. He started asking me questions while his guys waited to unload the trunks and put it on the plane. Shit I didn't have no answers. Finally

Simmons steps up and handles things. He gives them more gold and they load up the plane."

"What about Bobby?" Romeo asked.

"What do you want me to do?" Spooky asked.

"I want you to find out about Bobby, and be available. We've got some work to do." Romeo said and held a knuckle up to his lips, narrowed his eyes, and pointed a finger at Spooky before saying: "One more thing Spooky what exactly were you doing on Grand Cayman?"

"Simmons sent me there to keep an eye on Myrone."

FLORIDA

The Florida peninsula Chase reflected, was a long finger jabbed up the backside of the Caribbean. The finger's phony polished nail was he considered, Dade, Broward, and Palm Beach Counties. A diseased arthritic digit. He recalled how his life would never be the way it may have, if...

To anyone else seeking a getaway from a chilly climate South Florida remained a lovely pause in a snowstorm. Maybe a vacation condo or a few rounds of golf at a nice resort. Other than that with the crummy economy it was a cheaper way to enjoy the tropics and not need a passport. The pricier locales like Antigua, Barbados, St. Bart's, and the more exclusive destinations, could be for most Americans and Canadians alike not worth the airport hassles. Florida was an easy in and out hop for most North Americans. The TSA inspections, body scans, and pat downs, took a lot of fun out of a vacation, but a trip to Florida and filling the coffers of the state's merchants made for easier comings and goings. You could say that there was an epidemic of insouciance among airport security in Florida. After all the governor wanted visitors spending money.

It was a very large suite overlooking Biscayne Bay courtesy of the US Government. The Grand Bay Hotel in Miami.

"Agent Fuentes does have some fine taste," Romeo said as he inspected the three bedroom penthouse. He felt the mattress on one of beds, king size, and smiled. "I think this one will be mine," he casually strolled back into the sitting room and took a seat on one of the two sofas facing each other in front of a huge plate glass window overlooking the bay, and put his feet up on the glass coffee table.

Milton was still seated in a plush chair with his back to the window, staring at a ceiling fan, waiting.

Dina was still at the check-in when Milton and Romeo helped themselves to a lunch of the room's fruit basket, sodas, and nuts, from the mini bar. Turned on the TV and settled in.

The suite's door opened and Fuentes made her entrance. She moistened her fingers held them up and snapped, "Room service is right behind me with coffee so let's get with it. What do you have jet lag?" She took a seat, let the server place a cup and pour then dismissed him.

"What's the plan?"

"Chase word's out that our bad guy is shopping for a memory thief and a qualified orthopedic surgeon to do an extraction. He can't do it himself." Fuentes was sitting on the sofa sipping coffee.

"Why?"

"While you were getting cozy I picked up some information. Intel picked up word that our bad guy is on the move. An hour after Myrone tied up his bank accounts, his debt to the Russians tripled, and they want what they bought back." She placed her cup back on the glass coffee table and dabbed her full lips with a napkin. Leaning forward she resting her chin on folded fingers, her elbows atop her very shapely left leg.

"How do you know that?" Chase asked staring at her.

"Stop staring at my legs," She said pulling her skirt down and returning to the pose she'd struck. "From one of our Russian mob informants. He'd gotten himself dead,so the intel is the work product of a slow freeze. It was tangled up in a partially frozen deformed body we fished out of the Miami River." Dina Fuentes added.

"Partially frozen?" Chase said. "Who's he got lined up."

"We don't know who it is he has in mind, but he's going to send out his minions shopping for skilled labor. He will find you."

"Wonderful," Milton said glibly. "I can't wait."

"Would you prefer jail?" She paused for a beat, just long enough to remind him why he was there. "Listen we've dried up more of his funding, and suppose this memory he's looking to snatch has some serious bank accounts." She said.

"Who is it?"

"Who knows? Someone with knowledge of treasure or state secrets would be my guess."

"I bet you knew this all along. When we were in the Cayman's did you give Candella an extra push, as in fake ID and money?" She said nothing nothing at all just remained still smelling of rose petals and sexuality. "Listen Chase there's a potential snitch she's in Canada a friend of Romeo. She knows a little, but her pimp, or whatever, they were lovers, he was killed. That's the real deal. She was scared, her pimp was an old friend of Romeos. She called us wanting protection, and piece of the action in exchange for her cooperation. Before he died her pimp spelled out the name of our guy's driver."

"Who is she?"

"Her name is Yasmine, but the person we need is an employee of the man we want. He as in one Harold Spooky Pollack III 'his great grandfather was a famous sax player' is one very slippery old friend and business partner of the King of Africa." Romeo was in an adjoining suite eating a wonderful room service breakfast of bacon, eggs, fruit, and coffee, courtesy of the US government. Much better than prison food. Perhaps an encore would be in order, maybe a shrimp cocktail or caviar? He was sipping orange juice when the tap on the door broke his stream of appetizers.

"Who is Yasmine?" Chase asked. Romeo leaned back after reaching into the tray for a slice of melon.

"She played the short con in Vancouver." Romeo said.

"What did she do?" Milton asked.

"A rope with extensive experience, she was part of the old crew." Romeo said and sighed. "Aaa the good old days when honest crime paid," he said nostalgically.

"Crime never pays," Dina added.

"Please spare me the platitude you're a Federal Agent what would you know of the other side of things. We had some fine times." Romeo clasped his hands behind his neck.

"Tell that to her pimp Bobby Culture," Dina said. "He was killed."

"In Canada?" Romeo dropped his arms leaned forward and stood up. "How?"

"Unofficially?"

"I don't give a fuck, how!" Divine demanded.

"He was murdered." She said. "Black's bodyguard or whatever he is..." her voice trailed off when she saw the African darken.

The atmosphere in the room went from semi-casual to a den of hostility.

There was an aura of anger and hatred Chase had never seen.

"Romeo you're scaring me man..what gives?" Chase said softly. "Relax man we'll get the fucker."

"Bobby wasn't even a good bass guitarist. He was my brother. I'll kill that prick with my bare hands." He leaned his forehead against the wall. The only sound in the room was the clock ticking.

SECTION TWELVE

POOP SNOOPING

Through a series of eavesdropping, surveillance, and other sources, information was gleaned from Myrone. This was simple compared to other sorts of retrieval including but not limited to, serious arm twisting to the point of breaking, and in some instances dismemberment at one or another of the Black facilities. Intel was obtained and infiltrated. First by one very court-like order, totally fraudulent, to provide some useless information, and then a job offer for a convict.

The call from from Spooky Pollack regarding the whereabouts of Romeo Divine hastened his pickup and some words were shared. Dillings and Fuentes exchanged an immunity of sorts for Pollack's cooperation. He was right. This is what got Milton Chase a job.

In these times most diseases are cured electronically, the supercomputers and stem cells just plug in and some med tech can take away your cancer. But a broken bone needs a mechanic. I mean a real get your hands dirty kind of person. Someone not a afraid to get their hands in a pool of blood, bone, and gristle. No not one of those smart "generalists" what they used to call GPs or Internists of the 20th Century. They needed mechanics. Chase was a repairman.

Despite miraculous medical miracles, rejuvenated turbo charged nanotechnology and robotics, all the advanced intricacies in disease modification, people slipped and fell, broke bones, tore tendons, sprained and strained their basic frame. Fractures, tears, and wrecks, would always be part of the human condition. Not all of medicine required certified chess champion minds with advanced degrees in computer studies. He left the military gradually easing away from his commission via the VA, finally going full civilian, and setting up shop in the lull of treating the machinations of motion, the nuts and bolts of piecing together broken bones.

The Zen quality of day to day patient care soothed his unsettled recollections of war's nightmare. He served his country on the front lines and the Greater Good. War for him was done-but it lingered as those things do. Remorse paid its visits but never to a point of madness. No. There was a balance that came, and even though a sound, a blur or flash that caught his eye, he'd break out in a cold sweat knowing he could've done more.

Time and work smoothed things out and after a while things settled in his mind as he found his own brand of peace, and it made his life okay—even on that whacky drive down A-1-A staring at the arresting officer and the fact he'd been sent to prison for a crime he didn't commit. Now the mechanic worked for the managers in a world gone corporate.

DISORIENTATION AT A WHOLE NEW WORLD OF MEDICINE

Chase, the convicted felon, sat in front of the hospital administrator hyphenate, as in one particular lawless, loveless, and loony Dr. Maryellen Lowell. A once renowned however, defrocked plastic surgeon with more scars on her soul than most lesser surgeons had left. She smiled crookedly at him. Milton would recollect her expression as slightly playful, mildly amusing, and downright frightening with a hint of kink. It was the ping-ponging of emotions that caught him off guard. Watching her stare at his credentials, yawn, and become tearful was somewhat puzzling, but what the fuck. She was after all a whack job. As if his doctoring skills had more or less relevance than his military service; and the fact that he was a convicted felon was just window dressing. Add the part about being an escaped felon and that made her lean forward and say: "We can't pay you what you'd typically earn at a legitimate facility being unlicensed and an escaped convict..."

"Liberated, Doctor Lowell," Chase said. Maybe she'd been tweaked with some pseudobulbar implant who knew; maybe just going through a bad divorce. He handed her a tissue and put on his most simpatico constellation of body language, leaning forward, not staring but nodding slowly.

She artificially smiled. "Yes you are one of our special physicians."

"Maybe," She said. "I'm just an ordinary guy looking for work." He said.

"That's sweet." She sniffled. "We have some special benefits."

Hoping it wasn't along the line of sexual favors he said: "I'm in full compliance."

Chase was thinking about the fact that prison altered ones perception of their desires. The woman was not unattractive, but the thought of sex made flogging ones dolphin a bit more desirable than going through some artificial foreplay, and some series of emotional "shad roe of bad tuna" relationship with something beyond his mission. Well maybe once... he let his eyes drift.

No. He had the presence of mind to catch himself. There was nothing there but a crazy altered person. Something was really twisted about her Chase would later tell himself, subduing his prison stifled libido. No that chick isn't twisted, she's bent, and them some.

He continued: "You sound like a very nice person," Chase felt like he'd stuck a pair of fingers down his throat. "Maybe someday when our work is done we can hook up."

"Nice of you to say that." She said, wiping a tear from her face.

"But we have work to do."

"Along those lines, Dr. Chase, you must try to lighten up on the alcohol, specifically the fluids with Juniper berries.." Hallelujah. Chase got the job. He knew she was onto him when the plug was pulled on the Juniper. He got a job as an Orthopedist at one spectacular clinic in a city known mostly for its Hurricanes, glitz, and phony tinsel. It was a job for a convicted felon on a city sized campus, with a live-in hideaway from the law, sort of the unreal world he'd sensed in jail. Another institution.

IMAGES IN THE REARVIEW MIRROR ARE CLOSER THAN THEY APPEAR

Initiation day in the operating room at the hospital owned by the conglomerate of evil, who existed only on some ethereal plane was an odd medfix for Dr. Milton Chase. The scrubs a bit more comfortable than those of prison felt good against his skin.

The patient needed a total knee replacement. Some wetback asshole volunteered for free medical care, and a trip back to Venezuela. Not a big deal. The old fifteen minute scrub had been largely replaced by UV bacterial and viral enemies. That really didn't do it for Milt he liked the old drill. The scrub for surgery was a ritual of sorts, and the Betadine scrub gave him ponderable time to assess the surest dissection and focus on the procedure, the patient, and the implant. Not a big deal. They used to have vendors from the big corporations in the OR measuring and sizing the joint to be replaced. But now at the bad guy illegally run hospital for unlicensed criminal surgeons everything was done in house. The artificial joint would be created per measurements taken radiologically—what an ancient term—a sort of trans axial enumeration to the Nth degree, and no identification marker would show up on a tray. He was briefed on this before the OR nurse slipped him into his operating gown and size seven and a half gloves. It took him less than forty minutes to dissect, isolate, and remove the decayed joint of the seventy three year old man with degenerative arthritis. He was a diabetic and there might be some circulatory anomalies, but there was a stand by pancreatic machine. Great innovation. Made the Islets of Langerhans modify the input and output of insulin and glucagon, so that any mid operatory spike could be corrected. The anesthesiologist nodded and the joint went in, a simple gingylmus joint. Not rocket science just simple mechanics. The anesthesiologist seemed more interested in Chase than anything else.

After all, it was their first date and the guy passing gas was not your ordinary professional. He was addicted to his own medications, half for the patient the other half for old Norby Colligan. In the surgeon's lounge, more of a piano bar than anything else, the water cooler was filled with Vodka and the soda/candy/snack machine filled with an abundance of mind altering substances.

"Why all the dope and shit?" Chase asked, tossing his cap and gown into the trash.

"You can call me Norb."

"You can call me Milt, 'Milton Chase,' okay Norb?" They shook hands.

"You do good work," the anesthesiologist sat down. "You really don't need to do more than that. the bare minimum's all you gotta do. Just slice and dice and get the job done. That's all you've go to do to collect a pay check."

"What the fuck are you talking about?"

"We're all crooks or we wouldn't be here, right?." The anesthesiologist took a cup and poured a healthy drink.

"Doesn't the patient matter anymore?"

"Buddy, they matter. They matter a whole lot to the boss. I don't give a shit." He laughed falsely without mirth, and took a gulped from his cup.

Feigning ignorance and indifference Chase sat on the sofa and put his bloodied slippered feet on the lounge's table and said: "Our boss," he paused a beat before continuing, "We're workin' for the same guy right?"

"Yeah. The pay's decent and it beats doin' the laundry in prison."

"Been there, buddy," Chase said.

"Word has it you whacked someone," the gas passer arched an eyebrow. "Zat true?"

"What can I tell you?" Chase said. "I was set up. We were all set up, right?" Chase said. "Any gin around here?"

"Actually, no. The boss has some bullshit strict rules about the Juniper berry. Weird little fucker he is." Norb shook his head. "Weird as shit."

"That's cool. I've got some in my suite."

"Don't get caught with it, you could lose your job," he let out another phony chuckle.

"Odd that is, considering what we do here."

"That's interesting," Norb said. "Think about it, we're basically unemployable with incredible skills, and the only work after prison is in some funky hospital."

"The coinage is good almost too good." Chase said uncrossing his legs. "I'm grateful that I got the job, but I gotta wonder just what the fuck we're doing here?"

"Saving lives pal, especially our own." The anesthesiologist put his hand over his mouth and shifted his eyes from right to left. "There are some questions you just don't ask buddy."

"I reckon not," Chase agreed. "No, I reckon not."

"Yeah it's best not asking too many questions, just do our friggin' jobs, eh?" Norb started to walk out of the lounge.

"I gotta scrub in again, a total hip, then some hardware for a mangled dwarf." Nervous motherfucking guy. Probably raped a possum in some former life.

Norb stopped and turned to face Chase and said: "Good to meet you, Milt," he walked to the door pushed it open, paused, and said. "I'll be looking forward to working with you again."

SECTION THIRTEEN

D.D. CROSS

Woman Inside the Machine

Dina Fuentes had been at the facility for less than three weeks fully aware that it was a money laundering nonsensical place, where crooks got away with whatever they could because they were functioning under the general principal of Federal guidelines. It didn't matter because no guidelines existed here at this place of decadence. A place allowing physicians no matter what their past, to practice under the auspices of a facility catering to the hundreds of millions of groveling sick people.

In a city so racked with infirm it made a leper colony look like something of an ultra resort. Shit, Chase thought, after the C phone epidemic there was nothing but disease and charity hospitals.

The wealthy got more wealthy, and charity was a better investment than high grade diamonds. The wars needed money and the benefactors were the ultra wealthy—Milt's old patient clientele—Cosmetic Orthopedics. An entire specialty catering to those who didn't care for the shape of their bodies. Lengthening limbs, tweaking a toe, or straightening a gnarly thumb, it all fell into the nuts and bolts of his world. All the `what could've beens' that got tossed down the shit hole after that prick Dillings set him up.

Cool it, he told himself, stop ruminating and do what Romeo said to do. Romeo's orders, wishes, revenge were to take this prick down and get whatever you can. It might be a get out of jail free mission, but the pay was peanuts. This was an opportunity to make a little slush fund, a serious lay low for a few decades if Milton played it right.

Thanks to Myrone the accounts were already set up. Another country far from the wrecked, ravaged, United States/EuroAfrican/British Allies (USAEB) was a good place to leave as any. Especially if you happen to be a guy with a rap sheet. Even though Milton knew he could still make it as a doctor in the USEAB...why bother? Con school opened up new doors, new opportunities, and what once looked like the good life suddenly became not good enough. Milton Chase's objectives and aspirations trended differently lately. There were other ways to squeeze the shit out of life and enjoy every moment, and he intended on doing it

Especially in these times after the plague.

SECTION FOURTEEN

D.D. CROSS

THE PLAGUE

Lloyd Dillings and Dina Fuentes were pretending to enjoy a stroll along the New Miami River. They reviewed their progress on the case.

The place was filthy and they were forced to wear face masks to filter out the polluted air and horrid stench. Dillings wore a sidearm not just so the beggars might be less than inclined to panhandle, but he kind of liked to look like some bad ass law officer or cowboy. Dina knew he was a blowhard, and this was indeed a very bad part of town.

"Fuentes. You done good. We got Chase and that spade on our team. We got you the job on the inside and now all we gotta do is hope Chase comes up with the goods."

"Nobody has come up with the goods since the last outbreak, and that cost us as in half the Doctors available." She said.

"Well we got us one good one, honey pie."

"Dillings, I am not your honey pie."

"Your right sweet cheeks, but we got work to do and you better put on your little girl sweetie pie routine before going into the hospital again. They will kill you dead if you even smell of the law."

"It wasn't like that before the wars and the plague." She said. "Back then you'd be in a courtroom facing some sexual harassment charges."

"Good ole disease and war changes lotsa stuff, sweet cheeks."

The destruction of more than half of all physicians lives and the lack of medical schools, all victims of the wars, made seeking out even the least competent to be needed.

The people in power had an Occam's Razor sort of choice. The principle of parsimony whereby one should not increase beyond what is necessary. It needed little explaining that the number of entities required to explain anything. The fact that there were no more than a handful of docs and a whole lot of sick folks made it easy for entrepreneurial cads to come up with massive franchising from the government. The wars were not going well, and mall bombings and such were daily occurrences. So these facilities sprung up in cities throughout the US and the Greater European/African nations. It made sense that the simplest model is more likely to be correct especially when dealing with the unusual phenomenon of the times.

"If you got two choices go with the simplest one," she told Lloyd Dillings. "Pluralitis non est ponenda sine necceitate."

"They teach you that in lawless school, sugar?"

"No Lloyd, the world is in a crappy place that hasn't been seen before. It was William Occam who said it back in the fourteenth century."

"You're a bright girl."

"Woman, Lloyd, have you spent the last thirty years in a time capsule?"

"Excuse me ma'am. Woman it is. Jeez."

"Listen Dillings, we've got Chase and The King in this because of the demise of the guy in Palm Beach. The man <u>YOU</u> <u>KILLED</u> you know, the Sheik? Remember that? I'm not even sure if it was a legitimate sanction."

"Little lady! You saying I overstepped some threshold?"

"Enough with the sweet talk asshole. I'm not saying anything. Our job is to bring down Jet Black, and if you 'as my supervisor in the field' find something fit to be done I'll follow the orders. But if you're bullshitting me..."

"Hush on up. We are on the same side."

"At least it appears that way." She bit down on her lower lip.

"We are doll, we truly are." He held out a hand to pat her shoulder but she edged away.

"So my dear girl, we had that crooked schmuck Myrone who turned us on to some pretty flimsy banking maneuvers. A bogus lawyer who hipped us to the ties with the Ruskies, nice touch, but not enough. He even helped us divert funds."

"I'm still not so sure where those funds went."

"In due time, partner."

"And Yasmine?"

"Thass right pardner, that gal turned golden. She got us to her pimp—Spooky. Black and the little jigaboo, Mister Spooky, is gonna be the recipient of a huge cash reward. Why?" He answered himself, "because he's helping *us* out tying up the King of Africa and that fucking Chase to Dr. Jet *world's most horrific crime boss*. And then, the fucker ends up making the Russians want his head..."

"So we create a turf war, put Romeo and Chase into harms way and trash them?" She said.

"Thass right sugar, we burn the motherfuckers. We got us in the door of that skyscraper and Chase is gonna take us to the top of that building with that brainy coon Romeo who's gonna thaw whatever *special* things he got on ice. So that we are officially on the inside. That Chase boy is best being in the operating theater. He's fast and gets a job done just as quick as his ride back to the big house. That ain't too long a trip for that prick."

"You arranged a pardon..." Dina said.

"Honey, I arrange lots of shit. But lettin' that cocky little prick off with money to boot is not in the cards." Lloyd said holding his hand up to his mouth.. "Even if he lives through this it ain't gonna be pretty." Lloyd said.

"We'll see about that." Dina said.

"What are you gonna do call our superiors? Listen we gotta find out what this Jet Black has stashed away. And until we do that nigger and his Rapidthaw along with Chase under his arm at the medical facility is all we got. I just want you to know that getting too attached to the convincer ain't such a hot idea."

A DEN OF BRIGANDS

AT THE MEDICAL CAMPUS IN MIAMI

It was maybe four in the morning when Chase decided to leave his dorm room. A freaking dorm room—shit at least it beat prison and had a mini-bar. It was time to play with surveillance, the monitored hallways, and find out a bit more about this city within a city. Walnut General Medical Facility of Miami was in the heart of an intransigent society—a multicultural cesspool of sorts for refugees from about the world. Not only those affected by the Wars, but New EuroAfricans, Latinos had been there for centuries, and disaffected Middle Easterners all made for great studies of the uninsured sick. They were cast off by a government deep in debt to be cared for by a private sector that with a bit of motivation as in tax relief, and a bending of regulatory statutes, comply with the bare minimum to care for the sick suitors of an American Dream.

Chase loved to editorialize the fact that the country he served in the war didn't pony up jack shit for the vets, but forgave zillions in loans to ordinary street hustlers and miscreants. Shit. Prison cost the government more to keep him in a cage than to work on the poor people of the world.

So there he was locked in a still position outside of his room. The cameras were on him he knew that. He remained still until the realization that a purposeful attempt at checking on a patient might gain him access to some region taking him closer to the source. He had already donned his scrubs and jokingly made a full veronica for the camera. Fuck em.

Maryellen Lowell, the plastic surgeon who interviewed and hired him had an office a few blocks through the cavernous tunnels away, and that according to Norbert the gas passer was a good destination to start.

His gait the camera monitors would show was one of confidence, not stealth. Body language, facial recognition, along with scent melded together as an identification signal that could get one severely questioned, or legitimately through any checkpoint. And Dina, where the fuck was she sleeping? No, not tonight. This was a job, and Chase had less than a half hour to break into an office, swipe a Mempack or two, and get ready to show up without a hint of apprehension.

Unbeknownst to Chase, Simmons was fully aware of the dubious intent of the new hiree. He made it a point to bust this arrogant Chase and bring him to his master for a freeze and thaw party session. Would fucking this guy's dead aorta make him queer? Who gave a shit, he wanted him dead. Simmons wanted to be the man in the OR doing the big cases.

Chase strolled leisurely past a few orderlies grinning and making light of a late night set of rounds. After all he had performed several orthopedic procedures that day, and checking on his patients was not unheard of. Somehow Simmons knew he was heading in the direction of the administration structures instead of the patient compounds. Dark and somewhat hard to make out in the artificial light, he made his way through serpiginous alleys and corridors until a blast from an alarm sounded.

"Shit," Chase put his back against the wall.

The lights sprung on and within seconds a cart with two guards were in front of him—both staring at his ID badge.

"What brings you here, Doctor?"

"Rounds," Chase pushed himself off the wall and shrugged.

"You're going the wrong way."

"Really," Chase said, "I was going to get some workout time in too."

Simmons was hanging back in the shadows. That's good he thought, lets see what he's really up to? The boss would like that very much.

Simmons whispered into his wrist so the headsets implanted into the security men would get the message to let him pass.

Suspicious as he was, Chase proceeded and the guards, sans the visible Simmons let him go where he wished.

"Enjoy your exercise Doc," The robotic guard said.

"Just don't go hurting yourself."

Maryellen Lowell, MD, Director of Plastic Reconstructive and Implantative Surgery was what it said on the security lock door.

Thanks to Romeo, Milt had a needle sized device—smaller in fact than that—which he inserted into one of the sensors at the door.

Romeo was with his multitasking electropad and knew exactly what to do when the signal arrived. The door sprung a magnetic lock and disarmed the security system.

Chase wondered how old time jewel thieves did it-without all the gadgets. He went over to the desk and began going through its drawers, delicately at first, then a certain what fuck attitude kicked in, and he went into a full throttle rifling of the desk's contents. Time wasn't his good buddy, and he knew it, but he had to find whatever he could fast, and get his ass out of there. The lame excuse could come later.

Simmons watched his frenzied search through a crack in the door and wondered "What the fuck is this guy looking for?" The woman has nothing to show for her work, at least nothing the master would allow her to keep. Why would Chase care what she has in her files... Then it occurred to him, there was a log she kept of all of her surgeries. Her surgical schedules and procedures, all the patients she'd operated on, and what and when they were implanted. He had to stop Chase without really stopping him. If Jet Black knew he was setting this up his very nice position could be jeopardized. Call security again? No that would bring on too much heat. Have to think fast. Do something. Chase had already used one of Romeo's barely visible transmitting interpreters into Lowell's holo reader, and was looking at her daily operative reports in three D.

The holopad danced with blood and tissue and all the nuances of any operative report. But Chase saw something causing him to sit up fast. He jammed another transport reader into the machine.

Simmons saw him startle. Shit, he got scared. The boss isn't going to be happy he thought. This fucker Chase is trying to steal from us!

He walked into the room and fanned his hand. The lights came on and the holo shut down.

"Are you lost Dr. Chase?" Milton didn't know what to expect other than some unusual evidence that had already been transported to his confederate somewhere in Miami. Equally freaked out that Dr. Lowell had been implanting some very unsavory things into the bodies of the slave labor population. The lux of health care was in fact a fertile experimental hunting ground for sale to the highest bidders, and the Russian Mob and Jet Black had harvested an entire Fourth World of unintentional suicide assassins.

Romeo knew this now and could prove it. Simmons was in the middle.

"Hey, I'm just reviewing today's work. I couldn't sleep," Milt said, yawning.

"Bullshit."

"Maybe, but what are we going to do about it?' Chase dove to the floor, rolled, and came up behind him.

Simmons spun around. Should he just kill him? What will he tell Black? That he just killed the guy because he snuck into an office. No. Jet Black wanted this guy alive.

Chase swept his leg behind Simmons knees, the big guy fell, but not before pulling out his Freezare. Simmons took a fist to the neck and Chase kicked the arm holding the weapon and it fell to the ground.

"I'm leaving here now asshole." Chase said watching the big man pick up the weapon. He held his frame ready in case Simmons tried something. This time he was prepared to end him.

"I know what you are up to Chase." Simmons said timidly, recomposing himself, and reholstering the Freezare.

Milton stood erect Simmons, he estimated, had lost whatever adrenaline pulse he may have had, and been subdued. There'd be no more aggression from him, not now, not today.

The two men looked at each knowing there was some unfinished business, but both knew this wasn't the time or place to take care of it.

Chase raised his chin and retied his scrub pants. "Good then maybe you'll realize you're on the wrong side."

The two guards in the hall watched knowing that the spectrum of audio visual devices captured what had just occurred. Chase walked confidently back to his dorm room. He did not expect what awaited.

Dina Fuentes AKA the mysterious administrator in Bad Guy Land was sitting on his bed. She was back lit by the open mini-bar, sipping a very rare blend of water. "You're in grave danger, Chase."

"Is there any other kind?" Milton took a chair turned it around and sat in it.

"Is this another set up?"

"No." She said, and patted the bed for him to sit next to her.

Milton shrugged and sauntered over, dropping down next to her with a whoosh of the bed. "I guess you don't want the monitors to pick up what we're saying, right? Go on..."

"Dillings is no good. I know the guy's dirty," he said.

"I've felt that way since the beginning of all this. I just didn't have any hard evidence," she stopped and moistened her lips slightly. "Until now. I heard him talking to someone, he's in on something. I will get him on record."

"After the procedures I've been doing and what I just relayed to our pal Romeo, you might not get out of this either. So whatever you think you have, you'd better bust a move."

"I'm starting to get the general idea," she said. "There's a sense of urgency. I can feel it."

"You know the fact that you're in the room here with me is on every pickup screen Jet Black has, and you'll probably be marked as a government infiltrate. Or maybe they'll think you're coming on to me."

"I am a government infiltrate. Bringing Black down and shutting down this facility, here, in this town is my job." She pointed a jerky finger at him then buried it in the mattress. "Now this megalomaniac, Dillings, he thinks he's going to get rich off this." She leaned over him and set the glass on the night table.

Chase smelled her hair and felt her breasts brush across his body. He couldn't conceal the rush of excitement.

She crossed her hands on her lap and drew in a deep breath, "I think he's trying to rip off the Russians and Jet Black. It won't work. But nothing can stop him."

She ran her tongue across her lower lip and continued, "Black needs you especially now that he knows you're on to him. He's going broke, and the only way for him to get funding is through a derivative of Mempacks that only you and Romeo can obtain." She lifted her clasped hands slowly and let them fall back slowly into her lap.

"I get the idea," Chase softened a bit, bowing his head.

"They'll probably try to kill you." Chase said.

"No, knowing the way Black operates, it will be worse. Jet Black needs examples." She said.

"He also needs money." Chase said. Standing up he walked over to the mini bar, turned toward it and took a deep breath before returning to the bed taking a seat next to her. This time closer.

"Listen I didn't know you when we first met. I was wrong to have used the legal system to ruin your life, but this is bigger than that," she gushed. Her tone changed, it was shaky, on the verge of tears, yet soft, receptive. "But something happened..." she said, her lips parted slightly. "Would it be such a bad thing if I was coming on to you?"

"Some things still don't make sense." He felt her warm thigh against his. He looked into her eyes.

She leaned forward, exposing her long thin neck, held her mouth slightly open, lips parted. He smelled her breath and kissed her deeply. They fell gently onto the bed.

"You know some bad people are watching this?" He said.

"Then lets show them a good time." Despite Chase's fantasies there was not a yellow line bellow her navel that said <u>DO NOT CROSS</u>.

SECTION FIFTEEN

AN INVITATION TO MEET THE CHAIRMAN

Arno Puddamanjaro, age thirty three, was the first person from New Kenya to go to the US/EuroAfrican/ British world—his ancestors called it America. Now it was just another place on a frequently changing map. However, the thought of leaving the Continent for Miami was exciting. After a decade of bullshit he needed a break from the constant bombardment of what had become the triad's of the Continent. Apple, Google, and Exxon were the three mainstays, and the news had to be good every day. The fear that there would be spillage from the wars gave him that added wish to take a break from it all. His family were goat herders for thousands of years, and then he became a routing clerk for the very company he now enjoyed employment The Black Companies of the Greater World. Now he had to deliver a message to set up a meeting of sorts, and he would get a whopping credit chip that could take him anywhere in the world outside of the war zones.

Romeo and Chase had been in Miami with Dillings and Dina for less than a month. Chase had already taken his job and Dina had bipped in and out of the forbidden city leaving Romeo alone to his techno toys and schemes, when a very discrete attendant from room service indicated that someone wished to speak with the man wearing dreadlocks and was quite specific when and where. The room service attendant had no official affiliation with the hotel, nor did he have any official relationship with anyone except for the organization in Miami.

Arno was instructed to hand the note directly to the man with dreadlocks. No big deal. Of course Simmons had to remove his life before he could spend that credit chip. No signs of a struggle just a simple slip and fall.

Romeo Divine was set to meet with a very large man fifty miles north of Miami, in Boca Raton at Spanish River Park.

It was Tuesday at eleven in the morning. Romeo was instructed to wear a specific color shirt and sit on the beach, despite the watchful eyes of the monitors, and enjoy a smoke. Ordinarily a person of color would be under some scrutiny but Arno provided Romeo a sort of peace token which would imply that this was a man of wealth. It was a gold wristwatch of considerable value. Initially believed by Dillings and Fuentes to be some sort of honing device. Chase couldn't slip away from work but would agree that it was no big deal, after all; it was _they who could feed false information to whoever was listening.

  Simmons, Romeo would view as some Simian thug of a man. Gruesomely large hands with what appeared to be dirt beneath his fingernails made more for a bodyguard than the perverted Cardiothoracic surgeon he had once—albeit shortly—been. Nonetheless, the huge Neanderthal did indeed require Romeo Divine, King of Africa, to join his mentor and absolute Fuhrer to come on board with his incredible skill with the Rapidthaw.

"Look Romeo, I know who you are. I'm Dr. Simmons." He held out his hand.

Romeo did not reciprocate. He just stared at the mongrel. I know that you killed my brother Bobby in

Vancouver you fucking bastard. The time on your clock is running quickly, Romeo thought but said: "Then you know I can probably ruin your life with a blink of an eye."

Simmons laughed. It was a nervous, grating, mirthless, unpleasant sound, and as artificial as the implants he'd put in people's bodies.

The King of Africa feinted right then left, as if sparring with the minion of the arrogant evil, who hired Chase to work in one of corrupt clinics. Probably end up with another dead friend if I don't play this right.

"The job is a good one. The Chairman has something he will handsomely reward you with for helping him."

"The Chairman?" Romeo arched an eyebrow.

"For you I will refer to him as just that. A man among men. Look at all he has accomplished. Through his maneuvers he got you and that fucking loser Chase out of prison."

"I had the general thoughts that Dillings and his girl were not quite on the up and up."

"What do you consider the up and up? You are a criminal." Simmons said smugly.

"Perhaps I've made crime pay. But I never took nothing from nobody who didn't have it coming." Romeo said.

Get it together, Romeo was repeating to himself. He could feel the adrenaline rush, the catecholamines were flowing. The adrenal medulla was pumping dopamine, epinephrine and norepepinephrine, all under the mechanism of the sympathetic nervous system. This anticipatory state brought out the fight or flight response. Got to be cool. Think how it looks?

This was an adrenal crisis. Anyone with rudimentary knowledge of body language and reading a tell could see it. Be cool. Romeo called on his inner badness oddly calming his adrenal pituitary axis. The surge of epinephrine filled his muscles with oxygenated blood, the bronchi of his lungs open and ready to fight a lion in some primitive jungle. Blood pressure rising and diverting blood from his gut, sparing the internal organs from an attack. Ready to fight or fly, to toss his fists into the huge Simian body ripping his guts out. Control, Mon, he told himself. Keep the rage on the stage.

Romeo was an expert at the con and holding back the chemistry of his body was more mind over a well organized plan. Thinking quickly, more rapidly than the damned Rapidthaw, he bowed his head and shut his eyes so that Simmons could not see dilated pupils and enlarged jugular veins. Romeo knew Simmons was an MD, although not such a bright one. But this was not the time or the place to explode.

Despite his perceived ignorance of Romeo's elaborate plan, Simmons was on to this con. He knew Romeo was excited. He laughed to himself about it. Shit, even a moron knows that you can spot a potential customer by how excited they were, it was that outburst of epinephrine—how it constricts vessels in the skin and dilates skeletal muscle, dilates the bronchi increases glucose and raises fatty acids in the blood and shuts down the gut. This nigger was up for a job. What the eyes see and the ears hear the mind believes, and Simmons believed that he had one upped the great King of Africa with a job offer so thrilling that it made his adrenal cortical pituitary axis go wild. Damn nigger was gonna jump outta his skin.

"Calm down Romeo," Simmons said. "I know it's a career opportunity of a lifetime," Simmons held out a container of fluid. "Go on it's water. Have a drink."

Romeo inhaled deeply, smelled the container and took a careful sip letting the fluid remain on his palate a bit longer than usual. The careful observer would notice this suspicion. Romeo looked up and drank. Fortunately Simmons was less than a careful observer.

"I think I am a bit excited, Simmons. Who will I need to freeze and thaw?"

"So you're on board with us?"

"One hundred fucking percent." Romeo lied.

"Very good, the Chairman will be pleased," Simmons laughed again, the same grating, mirthless, fake laugh.

Out of nowhere the wind kicked up, and the sea exploded. White waves rushed the shore, and a gust blew across the sand uprooting the tree of a man, who burst into a blinding array of jabs to Simmon's face. Then a critical kick above the knee, snapping the bone like a twig, and several more blows to the man's torso. "Who do think you are?" Romeo shouted, shoving him to the sand.

The violence in the man on this desolate piece of beach took Simmons by complete surprise. He lay there amazed that this man could move so fast, and the next moment realized that one of Romeo's hands, its long dark fingers, were wrapped around his neck crushing his airway. Simmons watched him kneel and take pleasure in his power.

"Just remember mon, don't ever fock with me or mine ever again. Get it?"

The oxygen to Simmons brain was rapidly diminishing. He could feel the ache of the anaerobic metabolism kick in and knew that lactic acidosis was on its way and death might just happen here and now.

No, Simmons said to himself. He wouldn't or couldn't let it go that way. But he couldn't move at all. His thoughts became garbled. Lastly, before slipping away from awareness, he thought that there was no way he was going to ever let his boss know it ended this way. The words made no sense as he slipped further and further away into a darkness he had never known.

Suddenly, Romeo loosened his grip.

Simmons gasped as if emerging from a very deep pool of uncertainty. Romeo let him live to die another day

"I'm going to let you live for now," Romeo stood up and put his clenched fists on his hips.

This really is some powerful force of nature Simmons thought hazily. Sensing that the large African towering above him might really be the King of Africa. He started to rise.

Romeo planted the heel of his right foot on Simmons chest, and he spoke in a tone more powerful than the sea:"Don't even begin to think you can pull anything over on me EVER!" Romeo spit on Simmons. "Now you're MY bitch!"

Simmons lay there in pain grateful and somewhat surprised that he was alive. He shut his eyes, tears painted his face, and feces made a palate of his undergarments. When he opened his eyes the King was gone.

SECTION SIXTEEN

TROPHY ROOM

The real trophy room was in the depths of the salt mines. No one knew where the caves actually were, but when the two men rolled the crate into the very cold master chamber, Jet Black, wearing a very sophisticated body suit to maintain the proper temperature, grinned and instructed the workers to install his new treasure. A frozen entity collected from an Arctic Site in one of the ice chambers for further study.

Times had become difficult for the most evil man on earth; after all the freezing of his bank accounts made for a realignment of his finances, and a somewhat frugal running of a continuous criminal enterprise. His people were not getting paid on time, and every ounce of gold he had saved was misdirected to pay for his hobbies. Some of the bank accounts were diverted to some other entity perhaps a government not too friendly to his position. The wars, nearly a double decade rouse separated many from their funds. Nonetheless, a determined nemesis cropped up from time to time attempting to penetrate Jet Black's inventories. Numbered accounts, phantom corporations, and impossible tie ins made for a perfect invisibility. But it stopped. And who is it that can tie in all those entities,-no one he believed, except the bankers he used in Bern and the Isle of Man. His solicitor on Grand Cayman knew of him only by number, but was far from capable of manipulating his funds. However, his death would be useless if he could not reclaim his income stream. After all, these expeditions to remove frozen corpses were becoming expensive, and the reserves more difficult to sell on the open market. You couldn't exactly plop down a few gold bars and expect an eyebrow not to raise. Gold bars were plentiful but the encoded encrypted bank accounts gave him the fluidity to move in and out of nations without detection. The thought that someone penetrated his numeric fiduciary system raised his core temperature and made him sweat. He needed new secret accounts new hidden treasures buried, perhaps in the memories of his frozen trophies. Very rich and powerful people committed their secret encrypted accounts to a vulnerable, as if they would ever know, memory waiting to be lifted. New numbers and codes squirreled away a path to riches beyond his dreams.

But the techniques of mining those memories. Shit. The Russians were already on his ass telling him that without some pay on the horizon no more corpses of any meaning would show up.

Oh yes there was a remedy, Jet knew. With the help of his soon to be new arrivals everything would pan out fine. He needed the damned Rapidthaw.

From the Caves of Barbados to the Underground world of Portland treasures, art, jewelry, and cash would be found. South Bass Island just North of Sandusky held the secrets of one very deeply frozen Commodore Oliver Hazard Perry. The "We have met the enemy and they are ours," Perky. His early travels as a sailor took him to Europe and Africa during the Barbary Wars. Sure he knew where the money was. That whole mishap with his ship, The Revenge, was staged. He never climbed the ranks as fast as he wished. The fourteen gun vessel wrecked on a reef, while fulfillment of a mission to survey the mid-Atlantic coast failed. Although the court of inquiry found him blameless for the ship wreck. He took the time to survey another part of the world. A place where he began his Naval career as a midshipman aboard the sloop of war GENERAL GREENE in the Caribbean. Under the command of his father, Harlan Perry, a known bon vivant and rum aficionado, the man was largely rumored to have consorted with those privateers whose bountiful wealth had never been recovered. Yes, deep in the Quaker family's history was a an abundance secreted away from the ancient pirates of the Barbary Coast and the Caribbean.

He not only discovered the caves on the island in 1813, but managed to hide away treasures from his life of voyages in the calcium carbonate walls of the cave which lie a mere fifty two feet below the surface of Sea Bass Island the island. He did not die of yellow fever to be buried in Trinidad. He was right here in a crate frozen solid. His ship was blown off course to an arctic enclave of pirates. No one cared to inspect the coffin when it was moved in 1826, from Port of Spain Trinidad, to Newport Rhode Island, for another formal military burial. No, it was just politics even the statue looked like another human being. Before the war of 1812, Lake Erie, was a treasure trove for those wishing to make things vanish. The vast salt mines and hidden caves all of them mapped and logged for a time when, they could be retrieved unnoticed, lay in the memories of this very frozen Commodore. His public death was a sham, a new identity in Europe established, he set out to retrieve his fortune after the passing of his father. But, as things go, Jet Black knew they often miss the mark. He tapped the frozen corpse. "Make sure he is with the others and kept at the correct temperature."

Mapping his memories was flawed because he was frozen slowly, and a Rapidthaw something so vital to his work was, so far out of his reach. The damned thing was needed in the hands of a professional, or nothing would be worth anything. He smashed his hand against the cave's wall, and kicked the thawed corpses. "Dammit, where are you Simmons?"

Things Could Get Better

Jet Black knew that there was a US task force trying to infiltrate his organization. This came to him by way of one of his Russian affiliates, and the only way to infiltrate the infiltrator was to capture one and make some modifications. That is when a deal could be struck and a replenishment of assets would occur. He had what it took to manipulate one such agent already on his payroll, and with what he had in his ice vault might just bring him the means to satisfy his quest.

Location Location Location

Finding Dr. B's lair was a lot different than electronic fund transfers. It took satellite imaging and a scrupulous review of the unscrupulous images. Chase forwarded the info to Romeo en route. Transplanting diseased organs into healthy specimens was one thing, but the hospitals kept records which, thanks to shared data indicate the provider involved. Information on former licensees and their histories worldwide was not such a dutiful task for Lloyd Dillings. He knew who, and where, the quack killers hid and where they worked, drank, and drugged. He also knew where they traveled and all signs pointed in one direction.

Jet inspected the man with the gun and listened, unaware of who got him here.

"Put your hands in the air where I can see them." Milton Chase stared at him and said. "I ought to shoot you on principle alone you twisted fuck. You put diseased organs in healthy people. You reattached limbs on opposite sides on human beings, and made serious coin doing it all. You thought you could stash your cash in the islands. Guess what asshole? I want a piece of the action for the time I spent in prison."

"If I die today nothing occurs for you." Jet stared at the rigidity of Chase's flexor tendons on the trigger of an antique Colt .45, aware that he was only a burst of ATP away from a negotiation. "You have gotten to me."

"No shit."

"You have seen my wealth evaporate. Perhaps you helped to remove it. Nonetheless, I have assets only your dear Romeo can appreciate. I can regain my fortune with the help of your ingenuity and will share it wholesomely, and deliver your little police girl gone bad."

"No more bad guy bull. When I know that you've transferred all your dirty deeds, and dormant disease chains, I might not give a shit. You can return to 1 Sutton Place South and retire to a life of strip mining street walkers."

"You cannot change the spots of leopards but you can have some fun with them. As I will with Miss Dina."

"Listen good. I want Dina Fuentes back."Chase said.

"What will it take to do that?" Dr. Black said blithely as if he were some tool to be replaced. But he knew that time was running out along with the money. He needed to keep his generators going.

"The girl and some memories."

"Whose memories?"

"Yours" Chase said. "And lots of memories and lives returned."

Simmons entered the room and stood menacingly over the trio before Jet Black's desk.

"Can I put my hands down?" The bad guy said.

"Sure." Chase lowered his gun. "So we can deal?"

Jet grabbed an anuri needle and flung it at Chase. He held up his pistol, deflecting the mind altering deliverance device and rammed a letter opener through the top of his hand clear through the tissue to the desk.

"That's a pin job, Jet. Fuck with me again and I'll take another tool and ram it up your Johnson. You think you can turn me into a zombi just like that?"

"What's a Johnson, Milton?" Romeo asked.

"A Penis stupid." Yasmine said emerging from the shadows. She was a guest of Lloyd Dillings. Spooky had told him that Romeo had a soft spot for her. The fact was she could identify Simmons and Jet Black, as well as Spooky who was after all, in it for Spooky. Harold Spooky Pollack III, the legacy of a late twentieth century jazz musician, was not going to play anything, accept for both sides up the middle. Dillings being on the opposite side of Jet seemed at the time to be a good hedge. The bad guy winced and thought of nothing more than summoning his minions, but his messaging device was too far from his bleeding extremity. Chase dug the instrument deeper manipulating it between the third and fourth metacarpals. The two men locked eyes.

"You can do me no harm, nor will you. The girl and the prize will change your sphere of perception."

"The Feds of every Government got your number, mon, but the folks you set off to die are gonna want more than street justice." Romeo said.

"The rare ones who might survive." Jet said.

"Like I said man, give me the girl and we can make you rich enough to live in a world of gentle breeze, where large waves crest, begin to break, and scattered whitecaps occur at sea." Milt said icily. "Why bother with this shit, you've already corrupted most of the globe?" Chase said.

"Because I can," Jet said. "I can destroy the wind. By the end of the week my projects will make for a fear the world will never forget. Explosions and disease from a life of work. My work!"

"Come on man. Your bad guy days are over and you've got an out. Give me the files and features of the implanted subjects. Enjoy the breeze." Chase said.

"Fuck the wind! I have the key to the Kingdom of Earth. What I have in my trophy vault goes beyond anything anyone in this century could dream of."

"It must be a real beauty." Chase replied.

"Mon, on land the leaves and small twigs constantly move and light flags extend." Romeo added.

"A perfect retirement for a guy with your new disability."

"Your scales and charts, bah....Join me, come to my vault, and you will see what can trump all things known to the so-called civilized world.."

Chase twisted the letter opener evoking a screeching cry from the baddest bad guy on earth.

"Bullshit."

"This is what bonds my connections together. A common tie of the world and fear that the return of a leader with strength can arrive."

"You've already lost function of your hand. Let's lose an eye, or the hearing of an ear, shall we?" Chase said.

"Mon, you never told me about how wicked you could be?" Romeo added.

"As a doc I did some interrogation in the service. For this piece of shit-all bets are off."

"Keep the gun at his forehead but don't shoot. I want this prick to experience some agony before we play any further." Chase walked behind Jet's desk, pulled down on his left earlobe, and rammed a pen into his head."

"Freeze him, Romeo." Milt said.

"She's going to be on a plane." Jet stared at the juice lid in Romeo's hands. "Listen to me, Lloyd Dillings is a bigger cog in this than you could imagine. He's some kind of Masonic Nazi with connections to the Russians you may not wish to know about. I have the Mempack to prove it. But I also have the frozen body of secrets that can change the world and perhaps end the wars."

"Get everything you can outta this guys head." Chase said.

"Wait!" Jet said.

"Why?" Romeo asked.

"Come and see what I have collected. I will give you a chance to save your precious woman."

They boarded an ancient elevator and descended several meters below the underground cave.

"It took some convincing but here we are in your little den of brigands." Chase said.

Yasmine, Romeo, and Simmons watched the manipulator hold a bandage over his ruined hand.

"You might be able to do some real work here, Chase. I summoned you for this task and perhaps after you see what I have in store for you..." His voice trailed off. "Look around you. History is here."

There were several containers of bodies lined up in rows. Some ancient and non human, or human as we know them. Some prehistoric, and those identifiable in the uniforms and condition of their demise.

"They were all frozen. Frozen slowly with no Rapidthaw to salvage them." Black said proudly. "But you, Romeo, are the miracle worker."

They stopped in front of a cylinder which contained a block of ice. "Yes, yes, I keep the pH correct to maintain homeostasis."

"Is that who I think it is?" Romeo said.

"Yes it is. I need what he knows. My previous Rapidthaw failed on another subject. This one is the true prize."

Frozen solid in a block of ice was the body of Adolph Hitler. His limbs were horribly twisted, and Simmons tossed x-rays and MRIs displaying multiple injuries of the bones and cartilage.

"A man cannot survive these deformities." Chase said.

"However, he can be restored to a point of reanimation and memory extraction."

"How the fuck...He's supposed to have been dead?" Chase said.

THE REAL PRIZE AND THIS IS WHERE
THINGS GOT WEIRD...

In 1945 the Russians captured Berlin. US B-52s were pummeling the bunker, Adolph Hitler called home. It was agreed upon that the US would back off, and the Russians would capture the tyrant. Capture him and use him as an example of the horrors of the Eastern Front. Stalin wanted nothing less than to own that prick Schickelgruber's ass.

Hitler as well as his conniving cannibals had their own ways of diverting fortunes and misdirected the world. The takeover of Poland and reappropriating the funds of the Jews made for a wonderful windfall to perpetuate an obvious spent Reich.

It was in 1945 when the Russians did indeed capture Berlin. The so-called findings of the Reich Chancellery Garden showed a fallen leader doused in flames. Evidence in the possession of Russia's secret service would spell out to Truman at the Potsdam meeting on May 4 of that year. Yes, there were records from SMERSH, an equivalent to a black ops portion of the CIA, that the skull of Hitler was indeed absent of any gunshot wounds. A commonly used interrogation question used by the Bunker's groupies was that the Fuhrer shot himself along with Eva Braun, his new wife. It was indeed true that Sarkov knew of the stunt double found in the bunker. Plastic surgery and phony dental bridgework can easily be reproduced by any competent dentist. And Hitler had more than enough of those root canaling robots on his payroll. Even Hans Bauer, Adolph's private pilot, or Johan Rattenhuber, Hitler's chief bodyguard, didn't know that the Fuhrer had his own array of very private soldiers. SS men who would escort him to a plane, carry him to a port, and deliver him and Eva via submarine to a lovely South American hideout.

It was the prance through rubble, bombs exploding, that the husband and wife stumbled over. Even the hearty Aryan escorts couldn't withstand the blasts grabbing Hitler by his arm and forcing him toward an awaiting JU 55 Junker readied for a short takeoff. They met with a group of the 3rd Assault Army of the USSR. They shot the woman and whisked Hitler away contacting their chief of the 4th Subsection. Fly him back to Russia. This was the prize that Stalin wished for. Tempted as they were to beat this man silly, the Russian soldiers showed incredible restraint, retreating behind their own lines with Adolph Hitler in chains. He was put on a plane destined for Vladivostok when, the mechanical foibles of the day took the twin propped machine into a frozen stall fiercely pitching it into a barely thawing lake in the northernmost regions of the Soviet Union.

In the late twentieth century evidence in possession of Russia's KGB, was released to the world that Hitler did indeed commit suicide. A study of his alleged skull was absent of any gunshot wounds. Eva and dog Blondi had been autopsied proving that Hitler's demise was self inflicted, and that was that. Rumors and theories of Hitler's survival came and went, and the Neo Nazi mourners held up candles on his birthday.

The Chancellery Garden corpse fragments, satisfied the standards of any life insurance companies requirement for proof of death, and that was that. However, the one hundred year old sealed documents of the KGB tended to lean in the direction of skepticism to some scholars, but by then the world had become involved in a whole lot more madness.

"How did you come across this?" Chase gasped.

"My Russian friends enjoy the benefits of my work, and provide me with those things. You have stolen from me, yet you are capable of bringing to life that which is awaiting the refueling of my resources. In his mind are the memories of numbered accounts, stashes of artwork, diamonds and gold. Treasures the plunderer had taken. It was all about money the war of the twentieth century. Just money, and who knows what other secrets are held in that frozen skull. Watching him sit there in suspended animation would be silly, but fixing him would be much much better. My earlier works on other treasure troves failed horribly. But between you and the King perhaps a bargain can be made."

"For who?" Chase said.

"Look at the Femur and Acetabulem. If he's brought back he'll bleed out. That can be repaired, and it must be done quickly upon a Rapidthaw or nothing will remain but a deoxygenated corpse."

"So you want me to fix Hitler," Milton said.

"Or?" Romeo added.

"Die. You all die. Especially the girl, and all three hundred passengers, along with twelve city blocks."

"Nice options." Chase said.

"You can do this Chase. I know from my dear friend, and future cancer survivor, Mr. Dillings. My dear Mr. Dillings."

"And you, my Spear Chucking physicist, are familiar with the Rapidthaw to the point of perfection."

"Thank missa massah for acknowledging me."   The bad guy blew it off.

"Hitler was retrieved from the former Soviet Union. He underwent a gradual freeze and I do not have your ability to take his temperature down without destroying critical structures. Give him to me and I will turn over the records and files you desire."

Chase examined the options. Not many.

"Oh yes. fixing my own hand would be a nice touch." Jet said.

"You want me to operate on Adolph Hitler, save your twisted hand, and walk out of here not knowing what other seeds you're planting?"

"Well, we could all just die now," Simmons said. He was holding an ancient AK 47. He'd been laying low, looming in the shadows, and his voice rang out like sonic boom in an elevator shaft.

"Put your gun down." Chase demanded.

He pointed the barrel at Chase.

"Romeo," Milt said. "Can you thaw him?"

"Sure but he'll likely be some kind of mentally absent arbiter of what he was."

"Can you do it?" Jet Black asked. "Your life depends on it. I have implanted so many explosive devices in the bodies of unknowing suicide bombers that my role on earth is over. My genius is going to survive forever."

"I want the girl first." Chase said. "Besides, he's got to be thawed and stabilized before I can operate." Pointing his chin at the block of Aryan ice.

"Perhaps Romeo and his little woman will suffice as insurance of your return. I can await your outcome and consequent rerouting of funds before Myrone has a stroke, and the lung tumor I installed will take its course.

This can be deactivated upon your return and you can save another life. My driver, you know of him well, Spooky, he was on to you from the start. My very dear friend Lloyd Dillings did not blindly think his status would suffer by liberating a pair of cons like you and Romeo. Plus I will expect a superb reconstruction of my hand upon your arrival. I can wait. I enjoy the nocioceptive agony. Do not even consider involving any authorities, or anyone else. If you do many deaths, explosions, and diseases will await a world of unwitting accomplices."

"The whole thing's been a set up. Hasn't it?" Milton Chase said. Looking at Jet Black the way a good shit relieves a stomach cramp.

"If you hurry Dr. Chase, my driver will take you to my plane and you will have a connecting flight without a problem. Your security clearance from Mr. Dillings assures this. You will be on Dina's flight and perhaps recognize her. As for her, perhaps not."

"I'm ready." Chase said.

"As a show of good faith that you will not disappear someone will be available, if you survive the ordeal, to escort you back."

"Survive what? And who's the chaperone?"

"Danger is always met with surprise it makes our bodies work a bit tighter. And the chaperone? Ha. I think that will be quite the surprise. Let us call this task a test of your drive, to help reanimate our friend here. You will not fail."

"That dead Nazi isn't any friend of mine." Chase said.

"Me neither, Mon." Romeo added.

"Oh yes, Romeo, your friend might be seeking to save a damsel. You who have betrayed a friend, as in Myrone. A man who has stolen from me and will suffer quite heavily before his decay."

"Torture. I've had some fun with that." Chase said. "Listen, I'd like a Martini before we go. If you have no olives, just gin and tonic would be fine."

"You are quite mad. Madder than they said." Jet said. "Go now. Chop, chop."

"I take that as a no." Chase said. Simmons grabbed Chase's upper arm and shoved him into an elevator. Several miles above the surface they emerged to   find Spooky Pollack leaning against an awaiting cab. When he opened the door to the back seat Lloyd Dillings was smiling that broad smile, and those fat teeth glistened. "We got our work cut out, good buddy."

HE BROKE THE RULES IN THE LAND OF BROKEN RULES

Simmons opted for the liquor. Chase on the other hand hadn't had a tipple in a day or two. At this point of confusion Simmons needed something to settle the throbbing questions of what being frozen again might cause. Knowing what he knew would certainly get him in some sort of agonizing state. He rapidly pounded down two double gin cocktails, waited, and repeated the procedure. No way he would be frozen and Simmons was determined to keep it that way.

Simmons on the Rocks

When Simmons came into the room reeking of gin, Jet Black exploded. He grabbed a weapon and froze his Simian ass. Bastard breaks my rules he suffers.

Romeo was in the room patiently waiting for his friend Milton to return with the woman. He chatted briefly with the disturbed Dr. Maryellen Lowell, the twisted plastic surgeon, who placed explosive breast implants into the Federal Agent. Pleasant lass despite the weeping and all. He found the site of a partially frozen Simmons and highly agitated Jet Black amusing. The plastic surgeon was somewhat attractive Romeo would later recall, and realized prior to any advances that she was one sick, twisted, bitch implanted with, who knows what, sort of cooties, cancers, or other curiosities. Focking bitch could blow crazy anytime, he concluded, and left his amorous fantasies alone.

Several hours passed until the elevator doors slid open.

"Hey good buddies, we all came home to roost."

Lloyd Dillings. That son of a turd ushered in a crated Chase and a bleeding Fuentes, and said: "Get up nigger and thaw out your pal Chase so we can get the show on the road.

"Racial invectives?" Romeo had heard it all, but decided to let Dillings remain breathing, for now. "Sure," he said in that accidents can happen, and do, tone. "Sure."

Dillings ignored his comment and continued: "We got to thaw this fucker and grind out what this old Nazi has sittin' in his mind."

"Not so fast Lloyd," Jet Black said.

"Ah do believe that your need to live is just about up." Lloyd shot him in the chest.

"Mon you shot him just like that?" Romeo a man not familiar with being taken by surprise couldn't hold back.

"You catch on fast," Dillings said, waited a beat and shot him again before freezing him, "Toodles you sick fuck." He kicked over the frozen mess and then looked over at Chase. "Now we got to get on with business."

Chase was in a wheelchair of sorts, he had that statuesque Rodin pose, sans the pigeon shit, with the smartass grin unchanged from the airliner, where he'd just been transported.

"Thaw this bastard so we can get on with gettin' on." Dillings notched his chin at Chase.

"What if I'm not in the mood?" Romeo said.

Lloyd Dillings shot Dr. Lowell in the left eye. He sniffed the barrel of the weapon. "Gunpowder, love that smell. Gotta love it. It's gonna be `round forever. Ya know why?" Lloyd continued his smarmy toned rant, "I'll tell you why, it's because ever since old Mr. Nobel made up that vain, self-serving foundation, it's got to be around. There's some for her too," Dillings spit the words out and pointed the gun at Yasmine.

Romeo held up his hands. "Okay, okay, my mood's just right," he said.

Simmons, not quite frozen, his gin protected cells alive, watched the events unravel.

Dina Fuentes, her shirt bloodied, pulled a weapon out of nowhere and shouted: "Drop your gun Lloyd. I always knew you had some other agenda. I know now for sure you killed that guy in Palm Beach, and your going to pay for it, not this guy." She pointed her chin at the crated frozen Chase.

"You drop yours, little honey, I don't drop mine." Dillings said.

"Shit girl, you're gonna die here today. Almost died once today already," Dillings said it with a certain pleasure.

Simmons strained creakily to reach a freezing device. His partially frozen flesh oozed slowly as his lungs filled with fluid, but his will to react intact.

Romeo's arms remained in the air.

Finally Simmons fingertips found the switch. He sucked in a chunk of air and with all he had flipped the switch and gasped. "Fuck you, Lloyd!" his last three words gushed out as he froze Lloyd Dillings to hell.

Every cell in Lloyd Dillings body ceased to function. He was, Dina thought, an icicle dangling from a gutter. His eyes popped out as if he was begging for mercy, and the shit-eating sardonic smirk made him look as if he'd remain statuesque forever...

"I don't ever want to see your face again," she never wanted that image sitting in her mind's eye. She chose to shatter any chance of that memory forming a neurosynaptic path. A rumble began inside her ribs like a squall line about to spit out a twister. Just before the funnel formed and could rip through her flesh she took a deep breath, spun around, and delivered a blow with her right foot knocking him over, shattering Lloyd Dillings into a million shards of icy glass... "How you like me now, bee yatch?" She nudged a few Dillings bits with the insole of her left foot. "Have a nice meltdown you piece of shit," turned and walked away.

SECTION SEVENTEEN

Getting Back to Today

Chase had returned to the lair of Jet Black as an ice cube, thanks to Lloyd Dillings, the pseudo sky marshall, and all of his connections. Dina Fuentes was with him. There were dressings on the woman's chest where, Chase had made the incision all those thousand feet above Homeland Security.

After Romeo performed an immediate thaw on Chase, the first image he had was of Adolph Hitler's frozen corpse shattered into a thousand pieces. He was quite dead and Jet Black lay frozen, shattered, beside him just as Commander Perry. Jet's frustration, Romeo would tell him, just wasn't realistic. The asshole's greed for a restoration of the past just didn't work. But it was Dillings that hit him hard. "Looks like a lot of death going around here." Chase said.

"You are innocent, Chase." Dina said. "Dillings is dead. The greedy bastard who froze you after saving my life, and many others, set all of this in motion."

A FEW DAYS AFTER HIS DEEP FREEZE AND SOMEWHERE OFF THE BEATEN PATH CAFE

Romeo in a conspiratorial whisper said: "Milton, I have done something to save your soul." He stared at the freshly thawed Chase and continued, "I got to tell you, mon, I did a scan, a deep one, and know about the demons. I know about the shit you been carrying, the memories so fixed in your neural pathways. The ones from the woman, the bad stuff when she passed."

"Shut the fuck up,"Chase said.

"No."

"The war all that violent shit, too."

"Wait a second I can't remember, I can't recall anything, man-you fucking knocked out my pathways..."

Romeo tossed a packet of Cortichips toward MC.

Chase grabbed them.

"They're right here, go and study them if you want. But they're not inside of you anymore, mon."

Milton did just that, and a few moments later looked at the King of Africa and said softly:

"Romeo, I looked at the holo and shut it off. The memories are there in a packet, I don't have them any more in my head, shit-it's like I just had a dark cloud taken off my head. Do I want them back in here?" he pointed at his head. "Fuck no!"

"Hey mon, you never know, take some time." Romeo said. "See what does NOT fuck your mind."

"Maybe I can live without them, Romeo." MC held up the packet between his fingers. Maybe they're right where they belong. In a place where they'll be with me without being a part of me."

"Yes, mon."

SECTION EIGHTEEN

Chase's Former Life

Everyone's got a back story, and his wasn't without a loss that drove him. It sent him on a frenzied quest to forget- but never could clear his hard drive. The memories stuck. like an itch he couldn't scratch. He had nearly been married to whom, he believed the love of his life. They laughed at the same jokes, finished each others sentences, and made love as thoroughly as two people can merge into some Ameobic sprawl on the sheets. He was in his last year of residency when the nodule on the side of her thigh appeared out of nowhere. "Milton, I never had this before," she said: "What do you think it is?"

"Probably nothing." He examined it, transilluminated it, prodded and probed the thumb-tip size lesion. He thought it best to have it visualized and removed. "You know, honey, I can't do this, its not ethical, but one of the residents will." He thought it was a simple fibroma. But there is that always lurking suspicion. She was only in her twenties.

The pathology report came back as a leiomyosarcoma. The recommendations were a hemipelvectomy, the removal of not just her leg but the pelvis, as well. When she got the diagnosis Sheila said nothing, just a tear formed in her eyes.

"Honey, we can handle this," Milt said. "There is so much technology and resource available. "I'm on the cutting edge." Sheila, an anesthesiologist, opted for a simpler procedure, and took the last ramp off the life cycle.

Chase began hitting the bottle, but it wouldn't jibe with his life. With nothing left to lose he fought his own war against self-destruction, and decided to join in on the wars, and give his own life and anger for a cause. She died and part of him went with her.

He became the not so innocent, albeit dutiful soldier. After finishing his training he became the go to guy on the battlefield. As in finding the swiftest way to neutralize a combatant, and pull secrets from prisoners; at the same time, put together bullet riddled comrades. He was becoming more of a wreck. Years passed, and the love didn't evaporate. Maybe he could save some poor schmuck the horror of what he had experienced on battlefields, but many soldier's were irreparable. Chase tried not to live as another PTS (post traumatic stress) case, the best he could, but compounding his previous life, his way of working things out didn't work out well. He left the service.

Private practice Orthopedic Surgery. It was a new kind of challenge. The work put the man in a fancy sports car driving down the ocean on a Beaufort three day. A brief interlude from his dedication to fixing limbs, setting fractures, saving lives, the ones he could.

The wars were a lesson of sorts in driving, among other things, passing through pain. Private practice was a breeze compared to bombs and gunfire, and there wasn't much in the public sector that could rattle him. He enjoyed that life breathing in the good fortune of returning home whole, made him caress the steering wheel. He found some solace in silly things, like his car, and fixing a fracture.. He took what he could emotionally, but some things never left his mind, some thoughts were only a heartbeat away.

Life tippled on. He reconstructed a tumor ravaged body this morning, and it felt good. Life went on, or so Chase would say as he took pulls of booze from his ubiquitous flask at any occasion. He knew it would be trouble with the medical board if he was caught, but fuck `em. -He WAS a war hero there'd always be a way out. The imbibing wasn't celebratory, no, not at all. Rather a self-medication, meditation to stave off sullen sobriety. The Bombay Sapphire martinis washed away much of his recollections with a glow, albeit briefly. His memories didn't go away but stood at bay. Chase rarely showed any outward appearance of drunkenness. He'd figured out a way to keep his booze buzz going undetected by adding Adderall, a stimulant, to his daily blend. He picked that up in the military. Stimulants were furnished round-the-clock for soldiers and pilots on long missions. It had another name once, the so-called secret weapon-they called them Go Pills. They made Chase keep going.

But now, the memories were gone. The pain and sorrow lifted. Milton Chase felt as if some dark cloud had raised from his being. He was a new man and looked at his friend Romeo, and smiled genuinely. "I've had a brainscrub, haven't I?"

The King of Africa looked at him and said nothing. Not a word at all. There was a mischievous glint in his eyes. Finally he nodded his head.

"I thought you'd like these memories better when they're not sitting in your head, occupying space without payin' rent, and screwin' with your limbic system." He tossed another couple of Mempacks at Chase. "Here, I took them out of your head, too."

"I guess it worked. The brainscrubbing, I remember you telling me how sometimes people forgot to pay for the procedure," Milton said. "What do I owe you?"

"Nothin, mon. That was a freebie. Besides, I owe you. They look better in a box as a holo-flick, you can play with them if you ever really need to. File them, throw them away, do what you want with them, Milton. Put them where they belong, and leave them there."

"That works for me. I'll just sock them away in a place where they belong."

"I keep mine in the past," he said. "They just get in the way of things to come.

"What's next, Romeo?"